# FALL into ME

WILSON, NC

A note to readers:

It is strongly recommended that Book 1: Fall Into
Midnight be read first. Fall Into Me continues
the plot introduced in the trilogy's first book.

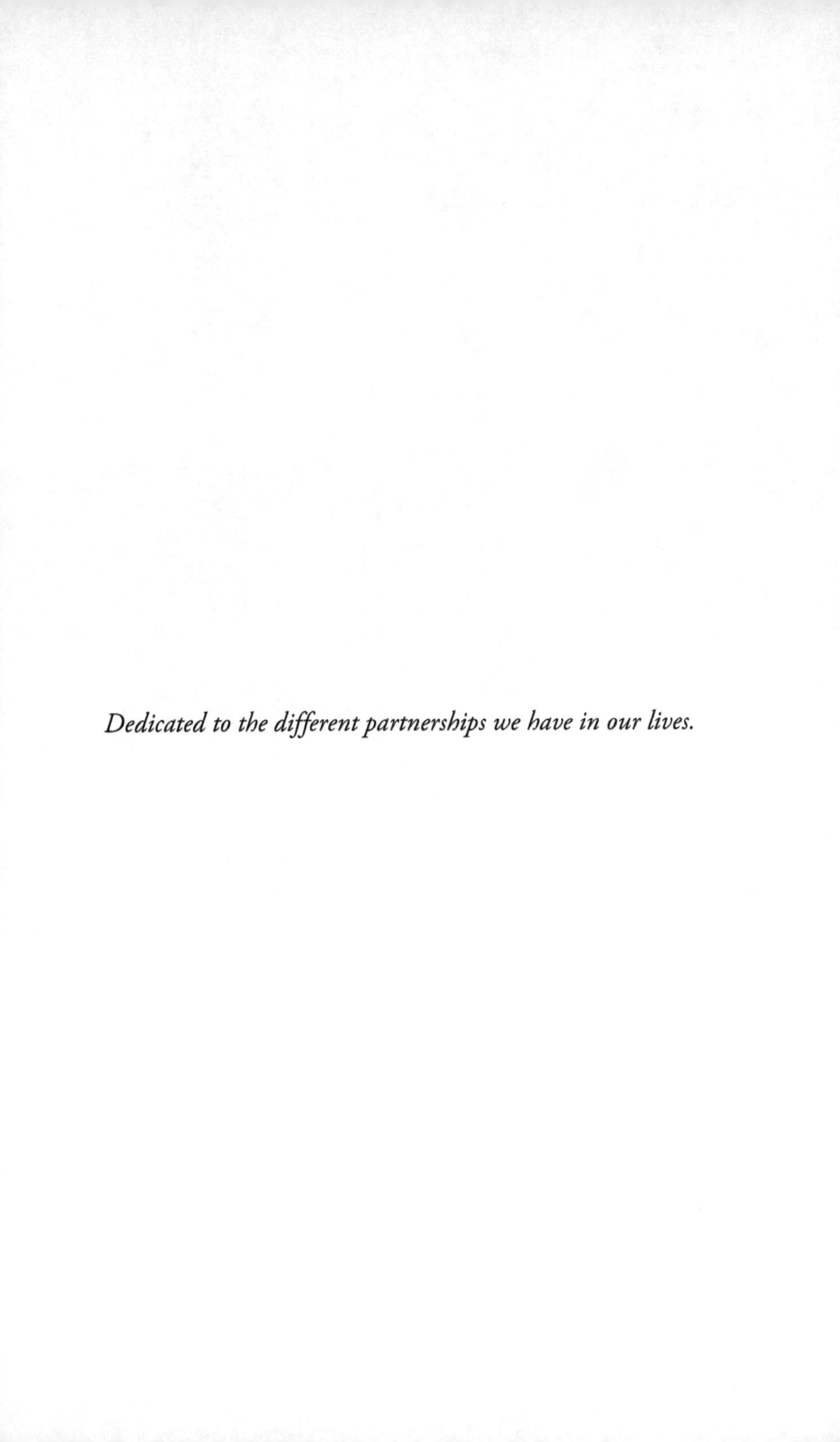

*Dedicated to the different partnerships we have in our lives.*

Scan the QR code below to enjoy the
playlist inspired by the book!

# CHAPTER 1

## Kee

"You're looking especially old today." Marcus stands before me at the threshold of Hannah's townhouse, looking fine as hell. He's wearing dark jeans that hug all the right places and a long-sleeved shirt that shows off his muscular arms and chest. He's been letting his facial hair grow, and a salt-and-pepper beard now highlights his sharp jaw. My hand itches with the desire to reach out and caress it. He looks good.

"You like it," he teases back, stepping into the house and shutting the door behind him. Marcus has come over almost daily to check on Gray as they've been healing over the last month, and he and I have continued to grow closer. He steps into my space, his right hand reaching out to gently hold my hip, and he kisses me quickly on the lips. Just enough to make me want more.

Bastard.

"Come to check in with Gray?" I ask, stepping back and regaining control of myself.

"I actually came to see you."

"Me?"

"Yeah, we've been dancin' around each other long enough, I'd say. Do you wanna go get dinner with me?"

"Like a date?"

"Yeah, like a date." Marcus shifts from foot to foot, giving away his nervousness. He's cute when he's nervous.

"I'd be down for that." I put him out of his misery.

"Tonight?"

"I can make tonight work. You can pick me up at my apartment at seven. I'll send you my address." I'm not one to fuck around when it comes to something or someone I want. I've found over the years that it's best to be direct and to let people know what I want. Sometimes, it works out great, and other times, men find it intimidating, and well, there's a reason I've been single for so long.

"Sounds great. I'll pick you up at seven. Wear somethin' nice," he says with a smirk. His hand still lingers ever so lightly on my hip.

"You mean my lovely suit and jacket won't do?"

Smiling, he leans in, his lips lightly caressing my ear lobe as he whispers, "I was thinking something a bit more formfitting."

Stepping back, he winks and walks out of Hannah's townhouse, giving James a wave as he passes the sedan out front.

Fuck, Marcus knows how to push *all* of my buttons.

Sighing, I shut the door and wander down the hall to the sunroom, where Gray and Hannah are lounging in the bright morning light. They've spent almost every waking minute together since Gray left the hospital. They're still healing mentally and physically, but Hannah's been with them every step of the way. Their relationship has grown stronger, and it's impressive. It's also kind of cringey. I mean, I love a good romance, but god, the amount of PDA is a bit much, even for me.

I peek into the sunroom and can't help but roll my eyes at the two of them cuddled up on the small loveseat.

"Who was at the door?" Gray asks without opening their eyes. Their head is on Hannah's lap as she sits at one end reading.

"It was Marcus, the old man who just stopped by to say hi."

Gray opens their eyes and turns to stare at me. "He didn't come to say hi to us, though."

"To me. Marcus came to say hi to me. Not everything's about you, Gray," I rib, giving them a big smile as I lean against the door frame, crossing my arms over my chest.

"Oh, so he finally asked you out, huh?" Gray has a huge smile on their face as they watch me.

Hannah sets the book down and starts paying attention to our conversation.

"You knew he was going to?"

"I may have had an idea."

"It took him long enough," Hannah says, smiling and picking her book up again.

"No kidding, I've been waiting for a month!" I can't help but smile thinking back to when Marcus was in the hospital and what it was like sitting with him all night, making sure he was okay after what happened with Dimitri. That was the moment I realized how much I liked him, and I swear it was the same for him. He would never admit that, though.

Sitting up, Gray grows serious. "Listen, just a word of caution. Marcus has been through some stuff with his ex, so he may not be super open right away. It'll take him some time, but that doesn't mean he's not into you. You'll need to be patient with him."

"His ex?" Great, the last thing I need is a grown-ass man caught up on his ex.

"He'll tell you about her when he's ready. Just keep an open mind, okay?"

I look at Gray closely. Marcus and Gray are very close partners; if anyone knows him, it's them. If Gray's telling me he's interested and I need to take it slow, there's a good reason for it.

"I got you," I say, nodding. "I'm going to switch with the grump out front. I'm sure he's dying to know why Marcus stopped by."

Hannah smiles at the mention of James and grump in the same sentence, and Gray shakes their head, laying back down on Hannah's lap.

Leaving those two to their cuddle fest, I head for the front of the house and out the door to switch with James. He's been stuck in the car for the last few hours and probably needs a break. It's been oddly quiet since Dimitri was arrested, and we're all on edge. We haven't seen or heard from Kiera in the last month and have lifted some extra security around Hannah. James and I are still here, but a lot of the other security has been detailed elsewhere.

"What did Marcus want?" James asks, stepping out of the black sedan. It's a crisp late-winter morning, and James has added a light coat over his suit jacket. He's looking a little worse for wear, with dark circles under his eyes, and his hair is messier than usual. I've noticed the changes in him since the last attack on Hannah, but he won't talk to me about what's going on. So, very typical James.

"He … um … asked me out on a date." I'm suddenly nervous about what James will think about this. He isn't one to discuss personal matters, and well, he kinda seems like an emotionless robot. We've never talked about our personal lives before, even though we've been partners for the last couple of years.

"Really? Wow, I mean, that's good, right? You like him." He almost seems confused and takes an interest in the far end of the empty street rather than looking at me.

"Yeah, James, I like him, and it's a good thing. I've been waiting for him to ask me out since we first met."

"You've liked him that long?"

"Yeah, I felt something the moment I met him. It has just taken us some time to figure out if that something was worth pursuing." It's interesting that James is suddenly curious about Marcus and me. But then again, we are partners, and I talk about almost everything else, so why wouldn't I talk about this?

"Well, I'm glad for you. It's good that Marcus finally figured it out." James shrugs and gently pats me on the shoulder with a slight smile. It's a lot of emotion for him to show, and even though he's trying to be reassuring, it has the opposite effect.

"Hey James, you good? Like, is there something going on with you that you want to talk about?"

"I'm all good, Kee." He nods, avoiding my gaze, and heads into the house. Sometimes, I wish that James and I had a relationship like Marcus and Gray's. They're open and caring toward each other and not scared to show vulnerability. All things that James and I lack. We've been partners for almost four years, and I still know almost nothing about him. I overshare with him to compensate for his lack of input, so he probably knows too much about me.

I miss the type of connection I've had with other partners, but maybe this is just how our partnership will be. I mean, it's been working for us so far.

# CHAPTER 2

## Marcus

oly shit, she said yes. I'm on cloud nine as I leave Hannah's house. I finally got to ask Kee out, and she said yes.

Fuck yeah!

I wave at James as I walk past the sedan and am rewarded with a short wave and curt nod. I walk quickly down the block to my own car and can't seem to keep the grin off my face. My beat-up, dark-blue Jeep is my baby, and even though she's been through hell and back, she still runs like she's new. Sliding into the driver's seat, I turn the key in the ignition and let my favorite Whitesnake song, "Here I Go Again," blast through the speakers.

My windows are down, and the brisk air steals my breath as I sing along with the chorus and drive away from Hannah's.

I'm in a good mood. I haven't dated in ages and something about Kee clicks. It feels good. It ... feels different. Everything about Kee is unlike my relationship with my ex-wife—from how we met, to how she makes me feel. I'm eager to see where this goes, but also cautious. I don't want to rush into anything, and I don't want to burden Kee with baggage from my ex.

Tapping my hands on the steering wheel, I head toward the office. I don't remember the last time I was in the office since Gray and I didn't come in while we were undercover at Club Midnight. I've had several weeks off from work to recover and debrief. Which means therapy—both physical and mental. I hate both. A small part of me hoped they'd forgotten about me there, but the call from my boss earlier in the week dashed those hopes.

I could use a longer vacation.

Pulling into the DEA office parking lot, I turn the ignition off and step out of my Jeep. The tall, mirrored building reflects the cloudy day back at me, turning my mood sour. Standing at the base of the building, I look up at it and can't help but wonder if this is where I'm supposed to be. It doesn't feel the same looking at this building. The usual sensation of excitement and pride is absent. A lot has changed since the last time I was here. I've changed.

Heading into the building, I dig out my badge, weapon, and ID for security. I look nothing like my photo. I look … older. Kee would love that.

"You're good to go. Have a good day, sir."

Nodding at the security guard, I gather my stuff and head toward the bank of elevators. Hitting the button for the 16th floor, I settle against the elevator's back wall and hope that no one else needs to get on. I'm not in the mood to shoot the shit with anyone right now. I want to get in, talk with the director, and get the fuck out. I miraculously reach the 16th floor without anyone getting on the elevator.

That's gotta be a first.

Stepping off, I take a moment to look around the floor. It hasn't changed at all. It's the same drab gray carpet, tan cubicles, and overworked people shuffling around from office to office. No one looks up as I walk in. I'm not sure what I expected, but this was not it.

Shoving my hands into my jean's pockets, I head toward the boss's office. I can see his tall figure from here through the glass walls of "the fishbowl," as we call it. He's on the phone, but looking up, his brown eyes lock with mine, and he waves me in. Opening the door, I give a tight smile and a nod before settling into the leather chair across from him.

"Yeah, thanks for the information. I'll pass it along. Have a good one." David Stevens, Director of the DEA, hangs up the phone and turns his full attention to me.

"I can't believe my eyes. Is that Marcus Wyatt? We feared you'd gone rogue and were working with the Ruez gang!"

"No, sir. Nothing like that." I chuckle and run a hand through my short-cut, graying hair.

"I heard about what you and Agent Alexander did and what you've been through. How did the time off treat you? Did your debriefing go well?"

"Yes, sir. Everything's gone fine."

"Loosen up, Agent Wyatt, you're not in trouble. I'm checking to see if you can return to work."

"Yes, sir, I believe I can." I glance at my calloused hands folded in my lap. Am I really ready though? I've been undercover for so long, following my own set of rules. Will I be able to fall back in line?

"Have you gotten any information on Kiera and her whereabouts?" I ask before I change my mind.

Stevens shifts in his seat, and I can tell he doesn't want to discuss it. "Well, we've gotten word that Kiera and Vlad have fled back to Moscow. We're assuming they're gathering muscle and gear. But it's been hard getting intel out of Russia, as you can imagine."

"By gear, you mean weapons. What do you think they're planning?"

Stevens shifts again. "We're assuming they're going to try to get revenge for Dimitri."

"What are we doing about it?"

"It's out of our hands."

"What? What do you fucking mean it's out of our hands?" I fight the urge to stand up and start pacing around the room. This makes no fucking sense.

"The U.S. Marshals have taken over the case and are managing it. We're in a supporting role, and they don't want our support."

"Sir, you've gotta be kidding me! You don't know Kiera like I do. She won't stop until she gets what she wants. What about Hannah and Gray's protection?"

"I told you, Agent Wyatt, we've been asked to drop off the case. It's up to the DA and the Marshals now."

"I can't fucking believe this." I run a hand through my hair and over my newly grown beard.

"You're really gonna shit yourself when I tell you this next bit." Stevens leans forward, folding his large hands over the stack of papers on his desk. "I need you not to make rash decisions today, okay?"

I stare at him. What could he possibly have left to say?

"It's about your dad."

Everything stops around me, and I feel a sudden weight on my chest. My ears start to ring. "What about my dad?"

"We were able to match ballistics from the scene of his death with weapons confiscated from Dimitri's club."

"You're fuckin' with me." I lean forward, holding my head between my hands, staring down at my denim-clad thighs and knees. "It can't be."

"We know your dad was working a gun and drugs case with detectives when he was killed. Dimitri has been active in the city for decades, Marcus. It's honestly not that surprising that they're linked."

"You're telling me Dimitri is responsible for my dad's death?" I can't seem to wrap my head around what Stevens is telling me. The ringing in my ears grows louder as my mind races.

"Yes."

"I want back on the case. Embed me with the Marshals, I don't care, I want in."

"I told you not to make any rash decisions today, Marcus. I need you to take a beat and settle."

"Don't fuckin' tell me to take a beat! I've been waiting decades to find out who killed my father, decades, David. Now I know, and I won't sit here and let Dimitri or Kiera get away with it."

"I can't authorize you to be on the case. You're too close to it."

Without another thought, I stand up, unclipping my gun and badge from my belt.

"I'm resigning as of today." I put both of them on the desk between Stevens and me.

"Marcus … think about this, this isn't how to handle it. We can work something out, so you get regular updates."

Rage burns through me, and I slam my open hands down on his desk, vibrating the glass walls surrounding us. I know people are watching, but I don't give a damn. "If you don't do something about this, I will, David. I can't sit here and do nothing."

"Marcus. Marcus!" Stevens echoes behind me as I storm out of his office.

Striding into the elevator, I can't control my breathing or the rage that's building in my chest. That fucker killed my dad, and there's still a chance he'll get away with it. I need to ensure that Dimitri and Kiera can never destroy another family.

Leaning my head against the cool steel of the elevator

wall, I close my eyes and take a few clearing and steadying breaths before opening them again. I'm going to go to Moscow. It's the only way to stop Kiera before she can do any more damage. I'll need help, though.

What about Kee?

Rubbing my eyes with the heels of my hands, I pull out my phone and send a message to Gray.

> I just quit. We need to talk ASAP.
> Meet me at the bar.

Gray's response is quick; they don't ask questions, and I know they have my back no matter what I decide.

> I'll be there in 10.

I jump into my Jeep, turning the radio off as I turn the key in the ignition. My thoughts are racing, and I know I need to get my shit together and my mind right if I'm going to do this, but fuck me. I can't believe that Dimitri was involved in my dad's death all those years ago, and now here I am chasing his daughter to fuckin' Russia. My knuckles are white as I grip the steering wheel. I'll be at the Public House Bar in a few minutes and need some semblance of a plan prepared that I can pitch to Gray.

I pull into the parking in front of the old brick bar that's been a staple meeting place for Gray and me over the last several years. Gray's bike is parked not far away. They're going to have to switch to a car soon. It'll be too cold to ride,

I think as I walk into the bar. Looking at our booth in the back, Gray has already ordered our beers.

"What's going on, Marcus?" Gray asks as soon as I sit down.

"Dimitri killed my dad."

"What?" I can see the shock all over Gray's face.

"I know, it's hard to believe, but Stevens said that ballistics confirmed a match with one of Dimitri's weapons confiscated in the bust."

"Marcus, what are you going to do?"

"I'm going after Kiera. David said she's in Moscow, so I'm going there. I will track her down and bring her back so she and her father can be prosecuted for the drugs and weapons they've brought into this city and the lives they've ruined."

"Marcus. This is some vigilantes shit you're talking about. You can't just go off like this and do your own brand of justice."

"I have to, Gray. I can't let them keep ruining families. They destroyed mine when my dad was killed, you know this. My mom never recovered. I can't have others going through the same thing I did."

"Marcus—"

"Gray! I'm doing it. I'm going. You're either with me, or I'll go it alone. I'd love for you to have my back, but I understand if you don't want to get involved. Especially now that you have Hannah."

"Marcus—"

"Don't try to talk me out of it. I'm going."

"Dude, if you'd let me fucking talk! I've got your back. I'm in. Let me know what you need from me and how I can help. But I'm not the one you should be worried about. What are you going to do about Kee?"

My beer freezes halfway to my lips. "I'm supposed to go out with her tonight."

"You should still go. Maybe tell her your plans or that you're going away for a while. You can't just ghost her, man." Gray's right, but ghosting people is what I'm good at.

"Yeah, I'll see how it goes."

"Marcus, you can't do that to Kee. It'll crush her. She's really into you."

"I'll think of something." I slam the beer back, letting the cold liquid calm the fiery rage in my gut.

# CHAPTER 3

## *Kee*

Marcus is late picking me up. Somehow, I feel like that's a normal thing for him. I look at my phone again and consider calling when there's a knock at my apartment door. I look at myself once more in the mirror and can't help but smile. I've pulled out all the stops tonight. I'm in a skin-tight gold bandage dress that hugs every curve of my body. Curves you wouldn't know I have given the suit I wear daily. My braids are down, the dark red tips popping off the golden dress. I smile to myself and go to the door.

Upon opening it, Marcus takes one look at me, and his eyes widen. That was just the reaction I was going for. "Is this fancy enough for you?" I ask, running a hand down my silhouette and resting it on my accentuated hip.

I watch as Marcus' eyes follow the movement down my body and know that I've got him eating out of the palm of my hand. Just where I want him.

"You look fuckin' amazing," he says.

"Do you want to come in for a drink before we go to dinner?" I've always been bold, but I'm feeling pretty forward tonight. I want Marcus. I've wanted Marcus for a while now, and I'm getting tired of dropping hints and playing flirty games. It's time to make a move.

"Yeah, yeah, that sounds good." I step back and open the door wider for Marcus to step through. He's dressed in black slacks, black dress shoes, and a dark-navy cable knit sweater that makes my mouth water with appreciation. God damn, he looks good in blue. I check out his ass as he walks in. Yup, that's looking pretty good, too.

I run my hand along his shoulders as I walk behind him into the kitchen. "What would you like to drink? I've got some whiskey, vodka, the basics. I've also got some amber beers in the fridge if you'd prefer." Marcus is looking around my apartment, and I can tell he appreciates the effort that I've put into the place to make it mine. It's minimal and modern, with pops of oranges and yellows in the furniture and decor. It's me, 100 percent.

"A beer would be nice," he says, sitting down at the island.

"How was the rest of your day?" I ask, opening the fridge and bending forward to grab a beer. I can feel his eyes on my body as I stand back up, opening the beer as I turn around. Marcus has a deer-in-the-headlights look about him, and I think he's starting to realize that he's bitten off more than he can chew.

"Uh, it was okay. I learned some stuff today that's kinda got my head spinning, to be honest with ya." Now that I look at him a bit closer, I can see the lines on his face clearer. He's been frowning a lot today. The furrow between his brows is deeper than usual.

"Anything I can help with?" I ask, leaning against the counter and pouring myself a vodka soda.

"No, I don't think you can do anything to help. I've gotta figure this one out myself." I look up from my glass and see him looking around the apartment.

"Who are they?" He's pointing to a framed picture on the wall above the TV.

"That's my family." I walk over to the large photo and point out each member, "These are my two older brothers, Darius and Jacob, and these are my two younger brothers, Shaun and Link. Then you have Mom and Dad, Sheryl and Joseph."

"You have four brothers? Damn, that's a pretty big family," Marcus says, walking up to stand behind me. I feel his hand rest lightly on the small of my back.

"Yup, they're a bunch of shits. They were always picking on me growing up, but I think their teasing helps me a lot in this job." I lean back into his touch, letting my body rest against his.

"I bet it does," he whispers, sliding his hand along my side and gripping my waist tighter.

"What about you? Any siblings?" I ask.

"Nope. No siblings, it's just me. My dad was killed in the line of duty, and my mother never recovered. She died shortly after, and it's been just me since then. My dad was a cop, and I always wanted to be like him when I was a kid."

"I'm sorry, Marcus, I had no idea." I look at him and see that his demeanor has changed, and I can feel him tense as I lean back into his body. I decide not to ask any further questions based on the way he responded. If he wants to talk more about it, he will.

"Maybe we go to dinner a bit later?" I ask, turning into his touch and looking up at him.

"I think that's a good idea." Marcus bends down, pausing momentarily before leaning in to kiss me. He's tentative at first, feeling me out before deepening the kiss, biting my lower lip as he pulls away. I struggle to catch my breath.

"Ah, fuck it," Marcus whispers, and before I can open my eyes, he picks me up and carries me over to the island in the kitchen. I wrap my legs around his waist as he sets me down softly. Our breath mingles with every rushed kiss. His hands are everywhere, running down my body, holding my waist, then caressing up again.

One arm around my back pulls me closer to him, and my dress rides up further as I hitch my legs around his waist. A groan escapes my throat as he kisses from my ear lobe down my neck to the top of my breasts. I've got a hand in his hair, and the other is desperately trying to remove his wonderful sweater. I growl in frustration as he takes a step back from me. I can see he's aroused by the bulge in his pants.

"Wait … wait … I don't know if we should do this."

"What? Why? What's going on?" I'm baffled and don't understand how we can go from undressing each other one second to stopping and questioning everything the next. "What's going on, Marcus?" I slide off the island and stand before him, adjusting my clothes as I do.

"It's just … it's nothing. It's nothing." He steps into my space again and kisses me harder this time. I can feel the desperation in this kiss and lean into it. I'm not sure what's going on with him, but I want nothing more than to help him find some peace, even if it's just for this one night.

I finally manage to get his sweater off and pull back to appreciate his body. Marcus is well-built, with a defined four, maybe six-pack on a good day and a trail of hair leading from his belly button to below his waistline. He's got a few scars that I run my fingers over before teasing them with my tongue. I want to taste every inch of him.

His breath hitches with every flick of my tongue, and I slowly kneel in front of him, undoing his belt, button, and the zipper of his pants. I can feel his eyes on me, watching every single move that I make. I open his pants and look at him, "Is this okay, Marcus? I want to taste you. Is that alright?" His eyes darken with hunger, and he nods, gathering my braids in his hands as I lean forward, taking him out of his boxer briefs and running my tongue from the base to the tip. His whole body shivers as I flick my tongue over the tip, licking the precum from it before taking him in my mouth. Hollowing my cheeks around him, I suck his length, reveling in the sound of his unraveling.

Marcus moans and whispers my name. He sounds … broken, and I like it. I want to be responsible for his undoing. I want him to lose himself in the sensations. I suck and lick my way up and down before kissing his flat stomach and working my way back up his body. He's desperate and pulls me up, kissing me harshly and fumbling with the zipper on the back of my dress. I give him my back so he can more easily remove the garment. I hear the zipper and feel its release as he slides it down, followed by his fingers and lips. He kisses his way down my exposed back to the top of my ass. Coming back up, he slips the dress off my shoulders, and it falls, pooling around my feet. I still have my heels on.

I smile to myself and lean back into Marcus' body as he continues to pepper my neck and bare shoulders with kisses. I press my ass into his crotch, and he groans into my ear. "You can't keep doing that," he growls, nipping my ear. "What? This?" I ask innocently, pressing my ass into him again.

I let out a small yelp of surprise as Marcus turns me around and picks me up, placing me on the island again. He hungrily devours my body with his eyes before kissing me as his hands caress where his eyes linger.

I need him badly. I'm dying to feel him. I reach for him as his mouth finds my nipple, making me arch into him. "Marcus." It's a broken whisper in the night, followed by a groan as he pushes my thong to the side and presses first one, then a second finger into me. I arch at the feeling and grip his hair in my hands as he continues to kiss, suck, and lick my nipples. "Marcus, please." I'm so desperate for him.

Pulling away for the briefest of moments, Marcus mutters coarsely, "Bedroom?"

"No, here, now," I say back, reaching for and grabbing him, pulling him close and gasping as he presses into me. He slides me closer to the counter's edge. Marcus runs the tip of his penis over my clit before pressing it at my entrance. Teasing me before slowly, god, so slowly, pushing into me. I feel like I'm going to burst into pieces already as he gradually starts moving. He's gentle at first, making sure I'm ready for him before he increases speed and pressure. Pumping into me harder and faster as I clinch around him. I wrap myself around his waist, trying to be as close as possible. As deep as possible. I cling to him and feel the sweat running down his back as he continues to fuck me.

"I'm not going to last much longer," he whispers into my ear as he leans forward, kissing my lobe and neck before finding my lips again.

"Not yet, Marcus," I plead, pulling him in for another kiss. I need more of him, all of him.

"Kee ..." It's a warning and a plea in the same breath, and I place a hand on his chest, slowing our rhythm before pushing him away from me.

I follow him down from the island and drop to my knees in front of him. Marcus' eyes follow my every move as I take him in my mouth again as I stroke and suck him. I hum in excitement as he leans forward, gripping the counter's edge. I know he's close, and nothing would bring me more pleasure than his climax. I open my throat further, and his cock hits the back of my throat as I gently cup his balls. His grip on the counter's edge tightens as he climaxes, and my name whispers from his lips like a prayer as his legs shake.

I swallow all of him, then lick and kiss my way up his body as he comes down from his orgasm. "Now, we go to bed," I say, smiling at him.

"What about dinner?"

"I think it's a little late for that." I reach out to him and lead him to the bedroom.

# CHAPTER 4

## Marcus

've been awake for hours, listening to Kee breathing next to me. I'm exhausted in the best way possible, but I know I'll have to leave soon. I need to be gone before she wakes up. It'll make it easier for both of us that way. It'll be better if she's mad at me.

I look over at her, sleeping soundly. She's lying on her stomach, her hair pushed off her smooth, soft back, and her head turned toward me. The blankets resting at the rise of her ass. I want her again; I ache for her, but know I can't. I shouldn't have in the first place. Not while knowing that I was going to leave for Russia. I shouldn't do this to her. She doesn't deserve it.

I run my hand down her spine, marveling at how the moonlight dances off her ebony skin. Fuck, she's gorgeous. If I make it out of this alive, I will have to spend the rest of my life making it up to her.

My hand stills … the rest of my life? What the fuck am I thinking? She's not going to want anything to do with me after this.

I roll to my side and slowly sit up, reaching for my boxer briefs and pants piled on the floor near the nightstand. I get dressed as quietly and quickly as possible, glancing behind me occasionally to ensure Kee is still soundly sleeping.

I grab the rest of my clothes from the kitchen and pause at the door. Should I leave a note or something? Will that make it worse? I need to go before I change my mind. Grabbing the door handle, I let myself out, ensuring the door locks behind me. I'll explain things to her when I get back. I hope Kee will understand why I had to do this.

I pull out my phone. There are three missed calls from Gray and one text message from about forty minutes ago.

> I've booked you a flight to Moscow for 10:00 a.m. today. You're going to be on your own when it comes to gear. Let me know if this works.

I start down the hallway, away from Kee and what could have been, while punching my response to Gray into my phone.

> That works. I'll be ready.

# CHAPTER 5

## Marcus

The bullet is close enough that I hear the air push away from it as it whizzes just over my head.

Returning fire, I use the distraction to run to the stack of box crates to my right and duck behind them as Kiera's men return fire.

I've been tracking her for the last week since arriving in Moscow.

I finally found her, but getting close enough to her to get revenge is the problem.

Kiera and her father have caused so much damage to Gray and Hannah's lives, to *my* life. Not to mention the other innocent people they've impacted through their drug running. Someone has to stop them. I never thought I'd be one to go rogue, but this seems like the only way to get anything done. There's too much red tape to go through the proper channels, and I want to see the Ruez family pay for what they've done.

A bullet pierces the wood beside my face, sending splinters fanning through the air. A few find their way into my skin as I recoil too slowly to avoid them. I've gotten too close this time to give up, but I'm outnumbered, outgunned, and almost out of ammo.

Every fiber of my body tells me to run, but my stubbornness makes me stay put. Perhaps I'll be able to make a move. Just a little longer. Maybe they'll slip up.

Looking around the side of the crates, I can see another set of them about ten meters up and to my left. I'll have a better angle if I can make it to that bunch. My gut clenches as I prepare to make a dash for better cover. I steady myself, feeling my heart beating wildly in my chest and my cramping muscles. If I'm going to make it, I need to calm myself and have a clear head. I take another deep breath.

A lull in the gunfire means they're either waiting for my next move or reloading. Hopefully, it's the latter. I burst forward from my position and make for the stack. I make it about halfway there when gunfire splits the air.

Pain blossoms in my upper thigh.

*Fuck.*

I feel myself pitching forward and to the side, as my leg gives out, sending me sprawling to the dirty concrete floor of the warehouse. My M1911 pistol flies from my hands as I try to brace for impact.

Rookie move.

I hit hard, taking the full force of my weight on my hands and knees as I catch myself enough to keep moving forward. I crawl, desperation and pain making it hard to breathe. I have to get to cover. Without my gun, I'm pretty much screwed. I know it, and so do they.

The sound of boots on the concrete floor means they're moving in, and I can hear them speaking in Russian as they start to surround me. Pulling out my phone, I text the location of the warehouse to the only number in it.

I hope Kee understands why I did this. I should have told her how I felt. It's too late now.

I take my belt off and make a tourniquet above the gunshot wound, hoping to slow the bleeding. Maybe give me a fighting chance. I get to my feet, feeling the world tilt as the blood loss hits me. I'm not going down without a fight.

I won't let Kiera win that easily.

I ready myself as the sounds of their boots grow closer. I manage to get into a low crouch while favoring my injured leg. If I can get the jump on them, maybe they'll be surprised enough that I'll be able to take them on. I have to be quick and concise in my movements from here on out. I won't have enough energy to fight if I get pinned.

The footsteps slow and then pause before moving closer to the crates I'm crouched behind. I don't wait for them to make the first move.

I step out from behind the wooden box and lay into the guy directly in front of me while trying to keep my back to the box to prevent an attack on my six. I manage to get Kiera's man in front of me into a chokehold, but it isn't enough, as he overpowers me with a sharp elbow to my ribs and a snap of his head. As the back of his head connects with my nose, I hear and feel the cartilage shattering and know my nose is broken. Pain and stars spark on my lids as I stumble backward. I can't see through the tears in my eyes, but I know I need to keep my hands up as best I can.

A blow comes from the right side, then the left, and soon, I'm on my back, breathing in the dust from the warehouse floor. Shit, this isn't going to plan at all. I roll myself into a ball and manage to protect my torso from the majority of the hits. I don't last long, and soon, the fatigue and blood loss hit me, making me dizzy. I start to black out, letting the fuzzy darkness on the edges of my vision grow until it overcomes me. As I begin to lose consciousness, I hear Kiera's voice as if it's being yelled down a long tunnel.

"Don't kill him. I want him alive."

# CHAPTER 6

## *Kee*

It's been weeks since Marcus disappeared from my bed. I can't help but wonder if it was something I did. Maybe I scared him away that night. I still wake up expecting to see him beside me, only to be alone.

I thought we had something, and I couldn't believe he would run after the night we spent together, yet I should have known better. I could tell something was off that night but decided not to push it.

Gray said he needed time to get his mind right to return to work. I don't believe them at all. Gray's a terrible liar and always has been.

"Penny for your thoughts?" James's voice snaps me out of it.

"Mind your own business, James," I say, getting up from the table and heading out the front door to take up my post across the street from Hannah's. I shouldn't be short with James, but I can't help my frustration. I need to figure out where Marcus is. I have a bad feeling about this whole situation, and I'm becoming increasingly frustrated and worried the longer he's gone.

Climbing into the car, I slam the door and turn on the radio. It's cold here, and the dreary weather does nothing to lift my even darker spirits.

We're still providing security for Hannah as the case against Dimitri is being built. As the DA's daughter, she's in almost as much danger as her father. We're all in danger, and there's no telling what Kiera will do to avenge her father. Hannah's dad—the DA—has been in protective custody since Dimitri's arrest and Kiera's escape and likely will be until the whole situation is resolved one way or another.

Fucking Marcus. What if something's happened to him?

I'm all kinds of distracted right now, and it's because of him. I feel disgusted for letting someone throw me off my game like he has. There's just something about him that puts me at ease, and I miss his goofy ass.

I can't stop thinking about his six-foot-three frame and salt-and-pepper hair. Not to mention how the skin around his eyes crinkles when he smiles and laughs and how he's so caring and gentle, while looking like he could kill you with a single blow.

*Ugh, Kee, snap out of it!*

I'm so gone for this guy.

I need to get Gray to tell me what they know about Marcus.

As I sit in the sedan outside of Hannah's townhouse, I can't help but wonder if Gray will tell me what I want to know. Marcus is Gray's closest friend, and something tells me Gray won't give him up that easily.

# CHAPTER 7

## Marcus

I come to as a scream rips through my raw and shattered throat. Everything hits me at once. I'm hanging from my hands, wrapped and bound by chains draped over a solid wooden beam. My clothes are gone, except for my shorts. My thigh is on fire, along with the other wounds scattered across my body. The worst is a large gash running from my belly button to my side. It's deep, and blood is still streaming, forming a pool at my bare feet which barely scrape the concrete floor.

I'm no longer in the warehouse, although this looks to be a similar location. It's hard to breathe, and I can't feel my hands anymore, so I've been hanging here for a while. I try to grip the chain above my hands to pull myself up and relieve pressure from my chest and shoulders, but I can't get my hands to work right. I'm cold, and it's slowing my movements down and making me clumsy.

It would have been better to have died than to be hanging in a warehouse completely bared for Kiera's twisted mind to play with. I feel helpless, and panic builds in my chest as I look around at the space I'm in.

In front of me, there's a table with a chair and … tools. Various things that cut, ply, stick, stab, and more, including a cart close by that has what looks like a car battery on it. I've seen these kinds of instruments before. They're used for interrogations; they're instruments of torture. I look at the battery and know precisely what that's for and can only imagine how thrilled Kiera will be as she electrocutes my ass.

I hope my last text went through. It's my only hope that anyone will know what happened to me. I hope Gray will understand what it means and know I'm in some deep shit. I've got to prepare myself for what's to come. If the text didn't go through, there's no telling how long it will take for someone to notice I'm missing and to come looking.

A door opens behind me, and Kiera's wicked chuckling sends a shiver down my spine, despite steeling myself.

"You're finally awake. For a moment, I thought maybe we'd been too hard on you!" Kiera walks into view with a Cheshire cat smile, stretching her face abnormally from ear to ear. If anyone is the embodiment of evil, it's Kiera. She has no moral compass.

"Good to see you too, Kiera. You're looking well." My plan is to keep it as light and silly as I can. That's what she knows me as. The goofy old guy from the club, I can play that up and hopefully use it to my advantage. The less she thinks I'm a threat, the more her guard will lower.

Make them think you're weaker than you are, Marcus. Rule number one of being tortured.

"Oh, so polite, Marcus. I wouldn't expect anything less from you. Did you know that you used to be one of my father's favorites? He absolutely loved your manners. The stupid old man let his feelings blind him."

She moves to the table, dragging the single chair out from under it and turning it to face me. Sitting, she crosses her legs and stares at me with hunger, interest, and disgust.

I stare back, keeping my face blank and as passive as possible.

I'm not a threat.

I need her to believe it. It's my only chance of surviving this.

A slow smile turns her blood-red lips up, forming more of a snarl as she runs her tongue across her top teeth. Reaching out, she runs a finger over the solid steel instruments on the table.

"Where shall we begin?"

# CHAPTER 8

## Kee

The sunroom at Hannah's house has become Gray and Hannah's safe place. They have spent almost all of Gray's recovery time here, and it's clear that neither is keen to leave anytime soon. I stand at the entrance, watching the two of them. Hannah is fully engrossed in her laptop and has no idea that Gray is watching her with the eyes of someone wholly gone. If Gray thought they had a chance to pull back, it's evident that the moment has passed.

They're completely gone for each other, and a part of me wishes I had what they have. Someone to always be with, support, and lend me strength when needed. I've had relationships in the past, but nothing like this. Nothing like what Gray and Hannah have. I thought that maybe Marcus and I could be something, but now I don't know. The longer he's gone without communication, the more confused and angrier I get.

Gray suddenly sits up, grabbing their phone, brow furrowing as they look at the message on the screen.

"What's wrong?" Hannah asks, looking up from her computer.

"I'm not sure yet." Gray gives her a tight smile and looks down at the phone again.

"Gray, what's going on?" I walk forward as the words leave my mouth. I can tell by the look on their face that it's bad news.

Gray looks from me to Hannah before showing us the phone screen. It's a text from Marcus.

His text has three numbers in it. Two are obviously coordinates as they look like the latitude and longitude of a location. The third message means nothing to me.

19019.

"What do the numbers mean?" I ask, moving forward. My heart is racing in my chest, and I feel lightheaded as Gray looks up at me from their seat on the couch.

"SOS. Marcus wouldn't send something like this as a joke, and given where he is right now, this can only mean that he's run into trouble and needs help."

*This isn't good.*

"What do you mean, where he is right now? What has he gotten himself into?" I've stopped at the table and have a death grip on Hannah's chair as I try to steady myself.

"Marcus took off about a month ago, as you know. What you don't know is that he retired from the DEA. He's only forty-two, but after what happened with Dimitri and the fact that the DEA wasn't willing to put Kiera on the Top 15 list, Marcus took things into his own hands. He also found out some shit involving his family and Dimitri, which sent him over the edge."

Hannah gets up and motions for me to sit. I can't breathe.

"I 100 percent supported him and backed his decision, giving my resignation as well. They weren't happy about it. Marcus and I had devoted our lives to the DEA for years, put our bodies through hell and back for them, and saw little reward. Mainly working on Dimitri's case. They were willing to let Kiera out of the country, knowing full well that she would take over her father's operations and efforts to silence witnesses." Gray continues looking from me to Hannah.

"Marcus followed Kiera to Russia, and I've been acting as his base of operations. I feed him as much information as possible and keep him on track. The fact that he sent this text means he is in deep trouble and needs help ASAP."

"I'm not saying this to freak you out, but he would only send this if it were serious. I'm going to have to leave you for a while." Turning to Hannah at the table, Gray puts the phone back in their pocket and stands up.

I'm too stunned even to know what's going on. Marcus went to Russia. What the fuck was he thinking?

"What? Where are you going?" Hannah's brows furrow in worry, and she tucks strawberry blonde hair strands behind her ear.

"Marcus is in trouble, and I need to check on him."

James suddenly knocks on the door. "Everything good here?"

"Yes," Gray says.

"No!" I shout, coming to my senses and getting up from the chair, "Marcus runs off to Russia to take on Kiera by himself and sends a cryptic SOS to Gray, who thinks they can just run off to save him. This is so fucked!" I'm on the verge of losing my shit at the pure lunacy of all this.

"You can't go alone," I say as silence fills the room, looking from Gray to Hannah and then to James.

"I'll go with you."

"Kee … I can't ask you to do that, plus you and James need to stay here with Hannah—"

"I'm going too," Hannah cuts Gray off.

"WHAT?" our voices all mingle as we exclaim as one.

"You sure as hell are not!" James bellows, crossing his arms over his chest as if that will stop Hannah.

"I'm going. You'll probably need someone with medical experience, so why not take me?" Hannah folds her arms across her chest, mimicking James' posture.

"Hannah, you can't. I can't have you there. I can't put you in danger like that." Gray is looking at Hannah, pleading with her, but Hannah's eyes are steely, and I know there won't be any changing her mind. "Tough shit, you and Marcus should have thought of that before setting off on this crazy crusade. We'll also talk about you quitting the DEA at some point."

I look to James. "James, are you in or out? We might as well take the whole fucking crew at this point."

"I can't let Hannah go with you two idiots. She'll never make it out of there alive." He gives me a smirk.

Sighing, I look at the three standing across the table from me. "This is a terrible idea."

"When do we leave?" Hannah asks.

"I need to add one more person to the team, and then we'll be on our way. Plan to leave tonight at 2100 hours."

"Who's the other person?" James asks, looking around at our little group.

"Luke from Midnight, you remember him?" A series of nods.

"Wait, are you telling me he's also with the DEA? Isn't he like twenty-three?" I ask.

"He's not DEA, but he is ex-military and has the necessary equipment and connections to sneak us into Moscow. He'll also be thrilled that you think he's only twenty-three.

It'll be good for his ego and vanity," Gray says, pulling out their phone and punching in a number.

"I'll be back in an hour or two, and then we'll start planning and prepping for our flight out. Until then, get your affairs in order." Gray nods to all of us before getting up and grabbing Hannah's hand before they leave the room. They need a minute, so I nudge James, and we head out of the room together.

"Are you alright?" James asks as we walk toward the front of the house.

"No, I'm fucking pissed, James. I'm angry for so many different reasons I don't even know where to start. How could Marcus leave for something so dangerous and not say anything to me? What if I never get to see him again? Ugh, I want to kill him myself!"

"Take a breath. We'll find him. Luke knows what he's doing." In a rare show of affection, James puts his arm around my shoulders and pulls me close.

"Let's go get Marcus back," I say, leaning into James.

# CHAPTER 9

## Marcus

My body is killing me. The pain is so much that I can't register all of it at once. Maybe I'm in shock. The bright side is that I'm no longer hanging, but the downside is that I think Kiera is getting bored, which means things are about to get even more enjoyable.

"You know, Marcus, I never pegged you as a man who could withstand so much. I've been having quite a bit of fun with you, but I'm afraid you're wearing my patience thin."

"So sorry to disappoint you, Kiera," I manage to gasp out around the swelling of my mouth and face. It hurts to talk, to breathe. I no longer have to pretend I'm weaker than I am. I'm actually weakened at this point.

"If you just tell me what I want to know, this could all end, you know? I would even let you go, I promise." She smiles slyly at the last bit.

Like hell she would.

"I'm afraid I don't have any of the information you're looking for, Kiera. I didn't have anything to do with your dad's investigation. I don't even work for the DEA, so I don't know what you're talking about."

"Please don't placate me, Marcus. It just makes me angrier."

Kiera nods to her goon, Vlad, and he wheels over the battery that now has wires connected to it. Once it's within range of where I sit, bound to my chair, he reaches down and picks up a bucket of water.

I brace myself as the water sloshes over me. It's fucking cold and stings as it comes in contact with all my open wounds.

"You know how this goes, Marcus. I'll ask you a question, and when you decide to stop being a smart ass and answer them, I'll reward you with a reprieve from our lovely little device here." She gives Vlad another nod, and he moves forward with the wires connected to the car battery as Kiera steps back.

"Wait! Wait! You haven't asked a question yet!" I yell, giggling manically as Vlad presses the wires to my bare chest.

Lightning races through my body as the electricity sizzles across my skin. For the briefest of moments, I might bite my tongue or chip my teeth as everything clenches. After that, there's only white-hot pain and darkness.

The pain starts over, and I can't hold my screams this time. They reach through my parched and ravaged throat and echo through the empty building. From somewhere too far away for my brain to fathom, I hear Kiera. "Again."

Kiera's laughter dances on the edges of my consciousness as I fade out.

# CHAPTER 10

## Kee

’m buzzing with anger, and it rolls like heat from my body. I can’t believe Gray kept this from me. How could they not tell me that Marcus went to fucking Russia and that he went after that psychopath alone! Gray, Marcus, and I will have a long talk when this is all over.

I’d want to kill him myself if I wasn’t worried about him. I need him to be alright, and I want him to be so we can continue what we started.

I want to confront Gray right now, but I’m focused more on the fact that Marcus is in trouble and needs help. He’s there alone, without any backup, and it will take us at least a day or two to get there. He’s already been missing for a few hours at this point, there’s no telling what can happen in that time.

I can’t believe we’re all going to Russia to help this idiot.

“How do we explain to the DA that we’re taking his daughter to Moscow to rescue a former DEA agent?” James asks as we set about helping Hannah pack. Ah, James, always the practical one.

“We don’t.”

"We can't just disappear with her." James stops what he's doing and looks at me. "You realize this is a horrible idea, right?"

"Yeah, I know, James. I just don't know what the other options are. I can't leave Marcus there on his own. I'd happily go with Gray, just the two of us, but Hannah's not budging."

James runs his hand through his hair. I can see the concern in his brown eyes. I know he's conflicted, which goes against everything he's been trained for in situations like this. Our job is to keep the principal safe, not drag them into more danger. James is always the one to reel me in and is the more realistic one in the partnership. This has to be driving him nuts.

"I just wish there was another option," James whispers.

"You know if we don't let her go, she'll find a way to go alone. At least this way, we can keep an eye on her."

James nods in agreement and continues to prepare, ensuring that Hannah's medical pack is well stocked.

"If it makes you feel better, James, I'm conflicted, too. I hate that we're dragging Hannah into a potentially dangerous situation, but I have to go. You know that, right? I can't leave Marcus there on his own."

"I know, Kee. We'll get him back." He reaches over and rubs my arm. It's the most affection I think James has ever shown in such a short period of time, and I appreciate it more than I can say.

"I'm going to go downstairs and check on Gray to see how securing transportation is coming along," I say, giving James a thankful smile as I head out.

Gray has set up a command center in the kitchen. The table contains documents, laptops, notebooks, and a coffee cup. Gray looks haggard already, and it's only been a few hours since they returned from their conversation with Luke. They've been on the phone nonstop since then.

Gray nods as I walk in, and their conversation continues unabated. It sounds like Gray and Luke are discussing flights and equipment again.

Hanging up the phone, Gray grabs the full coffee mug and takes a large gulp of the dark liquid.

"How's it going upstairs? Do you need anything?"

"Hannah's medical pack is well stocked, so I think we're all good there. Will you have the proper equipment for her, including a protective vest and tactical gear if needed?"

"Yes, I've got everything for Hannah. Luke will bring it over later so she can try everything on to ensure it fits properly. We should have everything squared away in the next hour or two. Luke's working with his former military buddies to get everything lined up."

"How is that possible?"

"They all served together, and now several run a security firm—Feather Flight Group—that does off-the-books work for the government occasionally. They've got everything we need, including transportation to safely get us in and out of Russia. That's if everything goes according to plan. They're also running an operation in Russia right now, so they already have a team there."

"Remind me to thank Luke once this is all over." I sigh and pull my braids into a loose ponytail to get them out of my face.

"Everything will be fine, Kee. I promise we're going to get Marcus back. He'll be happy to see you. He actually asks about you every time he checks in. I don't want to speak for him, but I think he misses you and regrets leaving without saying anything."

"Well, I hope so. It was a dick move. I probably would have been fine if he had told me what he was doing and explained it. I may have asked to go along, but at least I wouldn't have thought he ghosted me. It's been hard understanding why he disappeared without a word."

"I know. Marcus isn't the most thoughtful person all of the time. He does care, though. It just takes him a minute to realize it and act on it. We've been partners for years, and it took him a good year or so before he started opening up to me. You have to give him a bit of time."

"I hope I have the opportunity to do that, Gray." Just thinking about the possibility of Marcus being gone before we can get to him makes my chest hurt, and my heart seems to skip a beat.

"What if ... what if we're too late?"

"We'll get there in time, Kee, I promise. Don't give up on him just yet." Gray gets up from their seat at the table and wraps me in a warm hug. The buzzing of their phone pulls them away.

Gray nods at me with a sad grin and picks up the phone.

I turn and hide the tears that seem to have come out of nowhere. I need some space and head to the sunroom, hoping to find peace.

# CHAPTER 11

## Marcus

Kee runs her ebony hands down my chest, tweaking a nipple before skimming her fingers over my abs, down to the waistband of my shorts.

She sits, straddling me, grinding against me as her hands continue exploring. Her soft, plump lips nipping mine and then grazing my jaw as she kisses her way to my neck. At first, her kisses are soft, a caress, but they grow with intensity, morphing from pleasure to pain as she bites into my flesh. I try to pull back but can't seem to move.

"Kee, what are you doing? Kee, stop, slow down, baby."

"I want you, Marcus. Why did you leave?"

"I'm sorry, I had to go." Kee continues kissing and biting my neck and collarbone, causing more pain than pleasure.

"Kee …"

Wait … Kee isn't here.

I snap into consciousness to find Kiera grinding against my body, her claw-like nails dragging themselves over my bruised and battered chest. She's breathing heavily in her excitement. All I can smell are the stale cigarettes she's been smoking.

I try to lean away from her, but my hands are bound behind my back, zip-tied to the chair I'm sitting on.

Kiera's smile is one of a predator that has its prey cornered. I have nowhere to escape to and am completely exposed to her. I've never been this completely and utterly helpless in my life. This is what Gray must have felt when Kiera drugged them.

I try to buck her off and find that my ankles are bound to the chair.

Kiera laughs, leaning in and kissing my neck while raking her claws over my chest, leaving scratches behind with every touch. The only thing I can think of is head-butting her the next time she's close enough. But I don't get the chance as she sits back on my lap. She's too far away now.

"For a moment, I thought you were enjoying yourself, Marcus. You seemed to be having a good time until you woke up." Her evil smile and laughter make bile rise in my throat.

"Fuck you, Kiera," I growl. My throat is raw from screaming and feels like it's on fire with every spoken word, and my body is so weak I can barely keep my head up.

"I was trying to, Marcus. But you had to wake up and ruin all of my fun. You're always ruining my fun." She pouts and runs a claw over her lip before taking that finger and running it down the middle of my chest.

My skin throbs where the wires were placed. They've left minor burns everywhere that mix with the bruises and cuts left behind from previous sessions. I notice that someone has bandaged my side and that the bleeding has stopped. Smart. If I bleed to death, they won't get the information they need. Based on this, I know they won't kill me, at least not right now.

I have a little more time for Gray to get here. I have to hope that they are on the way. That is, if my text even went through. I have to believe that Gray is coming for me. It's the only way I'll survive this.

Kiera crawls off me and goes to the table, leaning against the edge of it while fingering the blade of a small knife. Her favorite tool, I've come to realize.

"So, Marcus, are you ready for another round?"

I can't help but swallow hard and flinch as she moves forward. My skin is so raw that even the slightest touch makes it sting. The thought of feeling that blade against my skin, slicing through it, is almost enough to make me lose consciousness again.

Kiera smiles, seeing me waver. "This can all stop. All you have to do is give me the information I want. I'll even let you go, Marcus. Let you get back to that woman you seem to be dreaming of. Wouldn't it be nice, Marcus, to be back with your lovely Kee?"

How does she know about Kee?

The shock must have shown on my face. Kiera's smile grows as she reaches behind her, pulling photos out of a large envelope.

"What is it, Marcus? Didn't you know I've been watching you for a while now? That's right. I've had my eye on your little group since Club Midnight's fall. I noticed that you and Kee seemed to have something long before the two of you even realized it."

"I'll make a deal with you. If you tell me where they're holding my father and when they're moving him for the trial, I'll leave Kee out of all this. But if you maintain that you don't have the information I want, I'm afraid Kee and my men might have to have a meeting."

"You leave her the fuck alone," I whisper, feeling murderous in my contempt for Kiera.

Her laughter bounces around the abandoned building. Echoing over itself again and again.

"How noble of you, Marcus. But don't you see? You aren't the one in control here. I am, and what I say goes. So. Are you ready to talk?"

Kiera stalks forward, blade in hand.

# CHAPTER 12

## Kee

"Luke was able to get us a flight out tonight. Does everyone have everything that they need?" Gray asks, looking at all of us.

I look at our newly formed team. We're all in our gear and ready to go.

"Luke's bringing the other tactical gear we need and will meet us at the airfield," Gray continues. They're in full agent mode, taking over the situation from the start. I'm grateful for that. I'm not sure I would have enough control over my emotions right now to make smart choices.

I watch as Hannah reaches for Gray's hand, caresses it softly, and see how Gray leans into Hannah for support. I think of Marcus' calloused hands and how they roamed my body, mapping every inch of it as if he had been committing it to memory. Maybe he had been.

Shaking my head, I grab my bag, turn with James, and head toward the SUV waiting to take us to the airfield.

It's been about eight hours since Gray got Marcus' text. My concern for him grows with every passing minute. I can't focus on that right now. I need to focus on the plan. Get to Moscow, set up our command base, go to the coordinates Marcus sent, find him, and bring him home.

We're all guessing that Marcus won't be at the coordinates he sent, which means we will have to track him down. It can't be that easy to find Kiera's establishments. Especially if she doesn't want them to be found. Gray insists that we'll be able to, and Luke already has someone working on it, but I'm still worried.

I let my thoughts wander as we drive to a private airfield outside the city. I have no idea who owns or operates the airfield, but those are questions for another time.

As we pull up, there's a large military cargo plane with the hatch open on the tarmac. Luke stands at the bottom of it, arms crossed over his broad chest. He's already wearing his tactical gear, and his long, grown-out blond hair is tied in a man bun. He looks different than I remember, not as youthful or goofy. He's steely, and as we pull up, I see he looks like a soldier prepared to drop into a war zone.

Stepping up to Luke, he gives me a sad, knowing smile and looks at our ragtag group, "Everyone have what they need?" he asks.

"We're all good here, Luke. What's our ETA?" Gray asks as we all follow Luke into the giant plane.

"It's about an eleven-hour flight, so we're looking to arrive in Moscow tomorrow afternoon. It'll give us a few hours to get acclimated and set up so we can hit the ground running with our search. We should also have locations for the rest of Kiera's real estate by then. Colter's been working on it for several hours and progressing well."

"Thanks, Luke, we owe you." Gray reaches out their hand, shaking his and patting him on the shoulder as he heads back toward the front of the cargo plane.

I have no idea how they've arranged this, and frankly, I

don't fucking care. I want to get to Moscow and find Marcus. I want to make sure he's safe so bad it physically hurts.

"You alright?" James asks.

"Yeah, just … nervous, I guess."

"We'll find him."

"I just hope we're not too late, James. He's been missing for a long time, and there's no telling what Kiera will do to him."

"I know. We'll find him, though, Kee, I promise." Smiling at James, I reach for his hand, and he grips mine in his as the plane takes off. I've never seen James like this before, and it's almost as confusing as my feelings for Marcus right now, but in a completely different way. We've been partners for so long, and I'm starting to feel like James supports me and is entirely on my side.

Leaning my head back, I try to close my eyes and get some sleep.

After sitting for several hours and still unable to sleep, I get up and head to the front of the plane to check in with Luke.

"We all set for when we land?"

"Yeah, the team will have two vehicles waiting at the airfield for us, and we have a safe house where we can set up base." Luke is in his element. The silly man-child from the club is gone, and he's all business. It's a side I suspected existed, but I'm still surprised. Impressed, even.

"You've done well, Luke. Thanks for arranging this. I don't know what we would've done without you."

Luke gives me a goofy smile. "It's not a big deal, Kee, it's Marcus. You know I'd do anything to help him out. I do have a favor to ask, though."

"Yeah, anything you need, just name it."

"I need you to put a good word in for me with James." Luke's smile widens as he says this and raises his eyebrows at me.

"Umm … in what way? Like you want to work with our security firm or …?" I leave the question hanging between us.

Smiling as the faintest blush crosses his cheeks, he gives me a wink. "Let's go with or." Luke walks away, leaving me in stunned silence.

Holy shit. What is going on? Does Luke have a thing for James?

I can't help but smile. James is going to lose his mind when he figures this out!

Walking to the back of the plane, I sit down next to Hannah and can't stop myself from grinning as I think about Luke crushing on James. James! Of all people!

"What are you smiling about?" Hannah asks.

Turning to look at her, I feel my grin growing. "I'll tell you later once we land."

"It must be good news, though. You're smiling like an idiot," Gray says.

"It's the best news, and you're not going to believe it, but you'll have to wait to hear it until later," I say, leaning back and crossing my arms. I look across the plane at James, who, as usual, has no idea what is happening around him.

"No fair! I wanna know now!" Hannah shoves me playfully, and I'm thankful for this brief moment of lighthearted fun, because I know the next several days will be challenging for all of us.

"Later, I promise. Gray, can't you do something with your girlfriend to get her off my case?"

"Don't look at me like that. I can't help you in this situation. You might as well just tell us," Gray says, holding up their hands and looking from me to Hannah.

Rolling her eyes, Hannah situates herself in the seat to be closer to Gray, who runs their hands through her hair.

"I think I'm too amped up to sleep," Hannah says, leaning on Gray's shoulder. I know precisely what she means. It's like my skin is crawling with the need to do something, *anything*.

"Focus on the humming of the plane and close your eyes. You'll be asleep before you know it," Gray whispers to Hannah as their hands clasp together. My heart squeezes with affection for these two people I'm lucky enough to call my friends. They're fortunate to have found one another. I can only hope that Marcus and I have such luck.

# CHAPTER 13

## Marcus

Unconsciousness would be welcomed at this point. Every inch of my body is in pain. My skin is one large open wound, and every touch, no matter how light, is excruciating, yet Kiera doesn't stop. She almost seems in a frenzy, like a shark, and I'm her injured prey, bleeding out in the water. I don't think she can stop.

I'm exhausted mentally and physically and can't help but wonder what would happen if I gave her the information she wanted. What would she do to me if I did tell her? Would she end it, let me go, kill me?

I know it's desperation making me think like this, but the pain is too much to bear now, and I need it to stop. I'm not sure if I can take much more. I'm not pretending to be weaker than I am at this point. I'm completely spent and almost out of the fight.

I'm not sure how much longer I can keep this up. It's hard to talk and breathe. I think I've chipped my teeth from clenching them so hard. My muscles are screaming, and I have too many open, bleeding wounds to count. I'm so exhausted that lifting my head off my chest seems impossible.

"Still with me, Marcus?" Kiera reaches over, grabs my hair, and pulls my head up to see my face. I can't see out of one eye, and the other has gone blurry. I don't know if it's from a wound by the eye or because I've taken one too many blows to the head, but it's getting harder and harder to see. To focus.

I snarl at her. Spitting the blood from my mouth and grinning like a crazy bastard when a bloody spitball lands on the front of her shirt—causing her to jerk back—is all I can manage as a response.

"Fucking disgusting as always, I see." She steps forward, ramming her fist into my bruised and swollen side. My breath catches as she connects with an already broken rib. I can feel it cracking apart and splintering internally with each hit.

I can't catch my breath.

Grabbing my hair again, she leans in close, her lips caressing mine, as her other hand runs down my blood-and-sweat-soaked torso.

"It's so sad that it's come to this, Marcus. I was really hoping we could come to an agreement. I would have loved to work with you in some way. I would have loved to do many things with you, with your body." Her hand keeps inching down until it's resting on my inner thigh.

"I'll give you another chance to tell me what I want to know, Marcus. After that, I'm afraid I won't have a use for you anymore." She digs her talons into the exposed flesh of my upper thigh, causing a gasp to escape from my split and chapped lips.

Smirking, Kiera turns, walking toward the table, and I jerk around as my chair suddenly moves in that same direction. I feel the tie around my right wrist come undone as Vlad brings my hand to the front of the table. He doesn't stop holding onto my wrist; he holds my hand in place as

Kiera picks up a mallet and a nail. Vlad pushes the chair closer from behind until I'm up next to the table.

"One last chance, Marcus. Give me the information."

Kiera places the significant spike on my hand, looks me in the eye, and brings the mallet down. Hammering the tip into my hand and crushing it at the same time.

I'm not even aware that I'm screaming until I run out of air and my throat closes. I can feel myself losing consciousness. The last thing I see before the blackness edges into my view is the nail embedded in my right hand and a pool of blood forming around it.

# CHAPTER 14

## Marcus

Throbbing.

Pain.

Throughout my entire body. My eyes flutter open as consciousness rears its ugly head. The pain makes me gasp, and I try to move but can't.

I don't think I'm in the warehouse anymore, but I can't tell. I think my eyes are open, but I can't see anything. Maybe they aren't.

Where am I?

The smell of exhaust suddenly assaults my nose, and I realize I must be in the trunk of a vehicle. I don't think it's moving, though.

I can barely make out the muffled voices coming from the front of the vehicle and know what's about to come.

This is where they take me out, execute me, and leave my body to rot somewhere in the remote wilderness of Russia.

Way to fuck everything up, Marcus.

I'll be another unknown body dumped in the snow. I can't believe I let myself get caught and that this is how it will end. How cliché of me.

I must be losing my mind. I can't stop myself from chuckling as the two men in the front of the car continue to chat about how they plan to dispose of my body.

I stop laughing long enough to realize that I'll soon be a corpse if I don't do something now. I have to get out of here somehow.

Wiggling my feet, I feel the rope give just a fraction of an inch.

Just a bit more.

I continue to rub my legs back and forth to loosen the rope and feel it continue to give.

One final flex and the rope gives. Scissoring my legs, I maneuver to pull them up to my chest, high enough to bring my arms from behind my back to the front.

I feel every single move that I make as the wounds across my body stretch and pull with my actions. Every inch that I shift sends lightning bolts through my body. My ribs are on fire, I can't feel my right hand, and my heart feels like it's beating irregularly.

Fuck.

Now that my hands are in front of me, I realize there's a thin hood over my head, so I can't fully see. I pull the hood off and use my teeth to break the tape around my wrists. I'm still a bit out of it and find myself chuckling as I'm freed. I'm having a hard time staying focused. I want nothing more than to simply lay back and take a nap, but I know I can't do that.

I am entirely free now and feel like I have a chance.

The vehicle starts to move, and every bump is excruciating. Most cars have an interior handle that will pop the trunk, and I've lucked out. This model has just that. Pulling the handle, I hold onto the trunk so it doesn't fly open, giving away my escape.

We're traveling down a remote dirt road. I can see snow drifts on either side of the vehicle and no other lights.

It's now or never, I guess.

Before throwing the trunk open, I get myself upright and mentally prepared for how bad this will hurt. If I angle my jump, I might be able to land in a snow drift, but that's not looking very likely. I hope I can jump and make it to the trees before they notice I'm gone. If they give pursuit, I'm completely fucked. There's no way I can move fast enough to stay ahead of them.

Throwing open the trunk, I brace myself against the biting cold and jump.

# CHAPTER 15

## Kee

"It's about fucking time." James sighs as we step out of the cargo hold and onto solid ground for the first time in about twelve hours.

"I couldn't agree more." I stretch, feeling stiffness in my lower back and legs. It feels good to be able to move about again. I take a deep breath and let the biting cold of the Russian air shock my system.

Gray catches up to us, one hand holding the strap of their pack and the other holding Hannah's hand.

"Let's hit the road and get moving before anyone realizes we're here."

"Tell me again how you arranged this, Luke." James looks back at Luke as he brings up the rear with a large pack and two large gear bags in each hand.

"Maybe over drinks sometime." He smirks, and I swear he winks at James, but maybe my sleep-deprived brain is playing tricks on me. I glance at James and catch just the briefest moment of confusion cross his face before he fixes it back to his stoic, emotionless mask.

"What else do we need to grab?" I ask, heading back into the cargo hold for any other equipment.

"There are three more bags of equipment back there." Luke directs us with a point of his chin.

James and I return to grab the bags as Luke, Gray, and Hannah head toward the two vehicles waiting for us on the tarmac. The black SUVs seem to be abandoned. There isn't anyone around to indicate how they got there or who dropped them off.

"What kind of shit is Luke involved in?" James mutters, picking up another bag that is clearly laden with weapons of various types.

"Suddenly interested in Luke, are you?" I ask, ribbing him a bit.

"Don't you think it's weird that he has access to all this, including a fucking cargo plane and a crew that can sneak us into Russia?" James either ignores the ribbing, or it goes completely over his head.

"Let's worry about who Luke is and what he's involved in after we get Marcus back. How's that sound?" I grab the last bag and turn to leave.

Hoisting the bags, we head back out into the groggy sunlight of the Moscow morning.

Gray and Hannah are already in one of the SUVs, Luke standing between the bumpers of the two.

"I'll drive one of the vehicles if you want to drive the other," Luke says.

"I'll drive. James, why don't you ride with Luke," I chime in before he even has time to think about it.

Luke gives me a small, sneaky smile, and I nod in acknowledgment.

So, I'm not losing my mind. There's something there for sure. At least on Luke's side.

James looks from me to Luke, seemingly confused,

before hefting the bags he's carrying and walking toward the second SUV.

Shaking my head, I drop my bag into the back of the blacked-out SUV and head around to the driver's side.

"Everything good?" Gray asks from the back seat next to Hannah.

"Yup, just giving the guys some time to bond."

Gray's small, knowing smile tells me everything I need to know.

I wait for Luke to pull out ahead of us and follow them as we leave the airstrip and drive into the countryside. We've landed several hours away from the outskirts of Moscow. Hannah soon settles in and is fast asleep as we navigate the morning traffic.

It takes almost two hours to reach our destination. It's a small, brick, historic three-level townhome that's surrounded by houses of a similar style. The street is quiet, and it will be easy to tell if someone isn't supposed to be there. We even stick out in our black SUVs.

Luke stops in front of the old brick building and gets out. He doesn't seem to be taking any precautions. At least it doesn't look that way from where I'm sitting. Gray must be thinking the same thing as me.

"Kee, why don't you let James know that he and Luke should go check out the building and that you and I will stay in the vehicle with Hannah until we get the all-clear."

"Copy." I slide out of the vehicle, looking around as I walk to where James and Luke are waiting.

"James, why don't the two of you check out the building? We'll wait until it's cleared."

"Sounds good. Are you all good? Armed?"

"Always." I nod and return to the building, leaving them to the task.

"How are you doing?" Hannah's soft voice floats up from the back seat of the SUV.

Looking at her in the review mirror, I give a tight smile. "I'll be a lot better once we find Marcus and I know he's okay."

Hannah reaches forward, gripping my shoulder and smiling. She hugs me from behind, capturing the seat back in the embrace.

James pokes his head out of the building, giving us a wave.

"I'll grab the bags. You and Hannah get inside," I say, jumping out of the vehicle again.

Hannah and Gray duck out of the vehicle, and I watch our surroundings as Gray hustles Hannah into the safe house.

I feel a huge weight lift when they pass the threshold, and I focus on gathering the bags, leaving two for James or Luke to grab as I head inside.

Once inside, I start to empty the bags on the kitchen table. Laying out all of the gear we've brought and sorting it by the individual that needs the equipment.

Luke and his team have thought of everything. We're a fully equipped team of operatives. We have tactical gear, weapons, medical supplies, and communication equipment. Now, we need to wait until nightfall to head out to the co-ordinates that Marcus sent.

Hannah and Gray head to the same room to get some rest. Leaving the three of us to sort out who gets the other two beds and who's sleeping on the couch.

"You've gotta be kidding me. You couldn't find a place with one more room?" James grumbles, looking at the space.

"I think we did pretty well, given our short time," Luke counters, sauntering over to the couch. "Don't worry, I'll take the couch. I wouldn't want your old joints flaring up." Smirking, he throws his bags down and flops onto the couch, all gangly limbs and sinewy muscle.

"The fuck did you say?" James snaps. "My joints aren't old, and I'm not much older than you. Wait until you're my age!"

Laughing at their antics, I head into the back room, closest to Gray and Hannah, to unload my gear and get some rest. If I can.

I haven't been able to sleep since discovering that Marcus was in trouble. I can only think about him alone, trying to survive whatever he's being put through. I hope we can find him in time. He and I have a lot more of each other to explore, and I've missed his humor and the soothing and calm side of him that only a few are privy to.

I miss the way his lips feel against mine, his hands on my skin, the way he whispers my name, almost like a prayer.

"Please hang on, Marcus. I'm coming for you," I whisper into the darkness of the empty room. I need nightfall to be here quickly so we can move. The longer we wait, the less likely we will be able to find Marcus.

# CHAPTER 16

## Marcus

Keep going. I have to keep going.

I can't feel my feet anymore. The snow and cold have completely numbed them.

I managed to escape Kiera's men, but I'm not out of danger. The woods I ran into must be part of a national park or something. There aren't any roads, no signs of life, and I've been walking for hours.

I'm lucky Kiera put my clothes back on before dumping my body. Otherwise, I'd really be fucked.

The cold is biting even with my jeans, boots, and sweater. Leaving me breathless every time the slightest wind blows. My lashes and beard are tipped in frost, and I'm afraid I might lose a few toes if I can't get out of here.

My right hand is purple. I'm not sure if it's from Kiera driving a stake through it, or from the cold.

Probably a combination of both.

Breathing into my frozen hands, I rub them gently together before carefully tucking them into my armpits in a sad attempt at warming them. I can't feel a lot from my hand, which concerns me, but also is saving me from that added pain.

My already broken ribs took a beating when I jumped from the trunk. My landing wasn't as graceful as I had hoped, and I hit the ground like a sack of shit. I managed to break some of the force of the landing by rolling into the snow drift, but the initial impact sent shockwaves through my battered body.

At least the cold is keeping the swelling down.

One. Step. At. A. Time.

I haven't been covering my tracks and don't think I'm being followed. I haven't heard anything to indicate that the two idiots in the car trailed me. Hence, it's likely that they've let me wander off into the wilderness to die out here. They may get their wish.

The wind picks up, and my steps falter before the toe of my boot catches onto something buried in the snow. I fall face-first into a snow drift and don't have the energy to pick myself up. I lay there on my stomach for a minute before slowly—so very slowly—rolling over to my back.

The sky is an ugly color of grey. Everything in this fucking place is grey.

I know I need to get up, know that the longer I lay here, the more likely it is that hypothermia will set in. As I lay, letting the drifting snow cover me, I start to lose con-sciousness again. I know it's happening, but I can't seem to move. I'm cold, but not as cold as before, which is a bad sign. I stopped shaking a while ago and know it's just a matter of time now.

I inhale a stuttered breath and let the sound of the creak-ing, bare, grey trees above follow me into unconsciousness.

# CHAPTER 17

## Kee

Darkness has fallen, and I'm ready to start looking for Marcus. The rest of the group is finally starting to rise and get prepared.

I'm antsy, and it's hard to be patient. We've lost so much time already that every moment from here on out is wasted. We need to hurry up and get out there. We need to find Marcus now.

"When are we heading out?"

Gray looks up at me as I walk into the kitchen, where they've laid out their gear.

"I know you're not going to like this, Kee, but I think I'll take James with me and have you and Luke stay here. We're just doing some recon, and I'd feel better knowing that we've got backup if something goes down. You're also too close to this."

"Too close to this! Are you serious? How many years have you and Marcus known each other? How am I the one that's too close to this?"

"You know what I mean. Marcus and I's relationship is different from the one you have with him, and I can turn it off when needed. Be clinical, if you will. I don't want you to rush into a bad situation like I did when Dimitri took Hannah. I want to do this right and minimize the danger the best I can."

I can't believe what I'm hearing!

I don't want to turn off my feelings for Marcus. They are what's driving me to find him. It's what's keeping me going.

"Gray, I'm going with you, and there's nothing you can do to stop me."

"Kee, please. I don't want to fight with you. I really need you to stay here with Luke and Hannah. *Please* don't fight me on this."

Before I say something I'm going to regret, I turn and leave the kitchen. Huffing in my rage and walking through the house, I end up in the small mud room at the back. Marcus and I spent almost every minute together as he was recovering. For the last month, I've been worried sick about him. Not knowing where or how he is drove me crazy. Now we're finally here, and Gray wants me to sit back and do nothing while they go off with James?

Gray has lost their damn mind.

Closing my eyes, I lean against the window, letting the cold pane of glass cool my burning skin. I need to calm down. Maybe Gray has a point. Perhaps I am too close to this. Would I be able to make the right decision if Marcus were in danger? I honestly don't know what the answer is.

I want to find him so badly that it hurts.

Leaning into the glass, I think back to when we were together. From the first time we kissed, how it felt having his hands holding my face, my hands, and caressing my body. He shared that his dad was a cop and that he always wanted to be one when he was younger. He loves being in law enforcement like his dad. Being a DEA agent was everything to Marcus, and the fact that he gave it all up to chase Kiera makes me even more worried for him.

Has Marcus forgotten who he is? Does he realize what he's done, not only to his career, but to me?

Does he care?

"Kee? You alright?" James walks in behind me, putting his hands on my shoulders and rubbing my arms. He does not show affection, and I appreciate his effort to comfort me.

"I'm alright, James. Just got a little overwhelmed and pissy with Gray." Turning from the window, I look at James. He's in full tactical gear and ready to go.

"Will you be alright staying here with Luke? I can tell Gray I'm trading out with you so you can go."

"No, it's fine. There's no need for that because I'm coming with you. I understand why Gray wants me to stay here, but if the roles were reversed, they would be the first one in line to save Hannah. I mean, they *were* the first one in line to save Hannah, so why can't I do the same for Marcus? I'm coming. That's the end of the discussion."

"You sure?"

I nod, crossing my arms and raising a brow at James. "Are you sure you want to go, though? You'll be missing out on some quality time with Luke." I smirk as James rolls his eyes.

"Not you, too. What the fuck are you guys talking about?"

I miss Marcus' humor and his ability to make everyone feel at ease. It's nice to joke with James and lighten the mood a bit. It feels good to bring some of that lightness back. I need it.

Walking back into the kitchen, I'm dressed in my tactical gear, just like Gray and James. Gray gives me one look and shakes their head. They may disapprove of me coming, but they can't stop me.

Weapons are loaded, and we look like we're ready to go.

"The plan is to approach the coordinates from the south. This will give us a clear line of sight into the bottom section of the warehouse. From there, we'll approach. The goal is to get in and out as quietly as possible with no contact. We don't know what we'll find when we arrive, but we should expect to meet resistance if Kiera and her men have set up operations there. Any questions?"

Gray looks around the room, taking in each of our faces.

"Alright then, let's head out. Luke will be here running the communications for the operation. If anything goes wrong, it'll be up to Luke to get Hannah out and inform the authorities what's happened. Luke, who's our contact at the embassy?"

"Greg Connor, he doesn't know we're here, but I've worked with him in the past, and if needed, we can reach out to him for assistance. He's former CIA and will understand what we're doing. His contact information is in your burners."

We all nod our understanding.

"Alright, if we're not back by dawn, assume something has gone wrong. Otherwise, we'll stay in touch and keep you updated on what we find." Gray pats Luke on the shoulder, nods to James, and reaches for Hannah.

We all leave to give them some privacy as they say their goodbyes.

I never got to say goodbye to Marcus. Hopefully, I won't have to.

# CHAPTER 18

## Marcus

Fuzzy. I feel faint and warm. I'm no longer freezing, but now it's almost too hot. I also don't think I'm outside anymore, but I don't know where I am. I don't want to open my eyes or see what fresh hell I've found myself in.

My eyelids are heavy as I force them open and look around at the dimly lit space. I'm on a single bed in the far corner of a small room. A wood-burning stove in the other corner is doing an impressive job of heating the space, and I've got at least three or four blankets piled on top of me.

No wonder I feel so warm.

I'm comfortable, though, and moving seems like too much effort.

Looking around the room, I see my clothes on a chair across from the foot of the bed.

Am I naked?

I peek under the blankets to see that I'm not entirely naked, as I'm wearing someone else's long-john bottoms. My wounds have all been cleaned and bandaged, which is impressive considering how many there are. If I don't die of some kind of infection, I'll be amazed.

I know I need to get up, move, find a phone, and call Gray, but all that is so much and takes a lot of effort. Right now, keeping my eyes open is taking all of my strength.

In the distance, I can hear someone talking in a soft tone. It sounds like a woman and a man speaking Russian. They're trying to be quiet, but I can pick out some of their words.

"He can't stay here."

"But he's hurt, and we can help him."

"It doesn't matter; he's all over the news, and they say he's a wanted criminal."

"Please, let him recover some at least." The woman's voice is soft as she pleads with the man to let me rest before they turn me in.

This motivates me, and I try to sit up, only to slump back under the blankets as my arm gives out from under me.

I'm too weak to do anything right now and need more rest before I try to get out of here. I hope they'll let me recover before deciding what to do with me.

I'm starting to slip back into sleep when the door creaks open, and a cooling breeze wafts into the room. I drowsily turn to see a man and woman entering.

"How are you feeling?" she asks in halting English.

"Fuzzy," I manage, my tongue thick in my mouth.

She nods, takes a glass of water from the man, and approaches the bed. Moving slowly and cautiously.

It's hard for me to lift my head enough to drink, and she has to help me as I take a few sips of the water.

I'm a bit more awake now, but still just so exhausted.

"You … are American?" the man says.

I nod and try my damnedest to keep my eyes open. They're just so heavy, and I'm so warm. I can feel sleep creeping in.

"American," I manage with a weak nod.

"What are you doing here?" the woman asks.

"Kidnapped," I say, deciding it's the best choice and explanation.

"I see," the man says, putting his hand on the woman's back and motioning for her to get up and follow him out of the room.

The fuzziness expands from my chest through the rest of my body, and I feel heavy, so … heavy …

# CHAPTER 19

## Kee

The warehouse looks abandoned. There aren't any lights on, and it doesn't look like anyone has been here in a while.

James, Gray, and I inch closer to the building, looking for signs of others as we get closer and closer. Gray tried their damnedest to get me to stay with the SUV, but there was no way I could sit close by and wait to hear back from them. I have to see it with my own eyes.

"Looks quiet," James whispers.

Nodding, we move to the front of the building. The old steel door is ajar, and the inside of the building is as cold and quiet as the Russian countryside around us.

"We move in slowly. Stay close to me, and if we run into trouble, we get out fast," Gray whispers.

James pats my shoulder, letting me know he heard. I return the move to Gray, and we move forward as one.

Sticking to the shadows, we move into the building, immediately taking cover behind a set of crates. Nothing stirs. There are no sounds other than our hushed breathing and the rasping leaves as their dried husks blow across the cement floor.

Gray motions to James and me, letting us know we're preparing to move to the next set of crates, giving us a clear view of the lower floor. A tap on my shoulder lets me know he copies the command, and I move, knowing he's my shadow.

Crossing the room, I get a brief look and can see faint signs of a struggle, and it looks like someone was definitely here at some point.

We reach the other side of the building, crouch down behind the crates, and look around the room, taking in the scene.

James points to the wooden boxes across from us that have been chewed up by bullets. A small amount of blood is on the floor where someone took some hits from the splintering wood. From there, we track the shots to another set of crates where more blood colors the floor red.

Nodding to James, we move as one to that location. He covers Gray and me as we crouch down to look closer at the containers and surrounding area. I can see where Marcus sat, where he put up his last stand, and where his body was dragged once he was subdued. The dust on the floor is disturbed and serves as a map, laying out the struggle at this location.

As I follow the tracks in the dust, I spot a smaller glint of plastic under some rubble.

"It's Marcus' phone," Gray whispers softly.

I bend forward and grab the small black scuffed phone. It's dead, but it's a sign that he was definitely here and was taken. I'm choosing to believe that he's still alive and was taken by Kiera. He has to be alive.

Gray turns to James, nodding to him, and he splits off, heading back across the room as I cover him from where Marcus made his last stand.

From there, we move to where we can see bullet holes from Marcus' return fire.

Moving to the stairs, we proceed to the warehouse's second floor. It's disappointing, as there's nothing significant and nothing to give us any information about where they may have taken Marcus. There's nothing there that's relevant to our search. The only signs of anyone in the warehouse are bullet holes and blood stains on the first floor.

*God damn it, Marcus, you've really fucked yourself over this time.*

Shaking my head in disappointment, I follow James and Gray as we head back down to the bottom floor, doing one more sweep before we move back to the door. Returning into the open night, we disappear into the shadows and return to the SUV.

We sit silently before James starts the vehicle and navigates back to the main road.

"What now?" His voice is barely audible as the heaviness sets in between us. "That was a lot of blood."

"We'll charge Marcus' phone and see if we can find anything from there. Maybe Luke's friends will have found more information about the buildings that Kiera owns, which will give us some leads."

"Sounds good."

"Wait, do you see those tracks?" My voice is high with excitement as I spot the tire tracks turning down the opposite direction of the road.

James and Gray both look to the left. "It just snowed, so the tracks must be fresh," I whisper breathlessly.

"Fuck, me," James whispers.

"Follow the tracks, take it slow, and keep your eyes peeled for where they turn off," Gray orders, and James turns to follow the tracks before they even finish their sentence.

I lean forward in my seat to see better.

We've been on the road for about fifteen minutes when we all exclaim simultaneously, "There!" Gray says, and I shout, "Stop!" The tracks turn off the road to the left, and we can see them continuing down a dark road leading into the snow-covered forest.

We're frozen briefly before James pushes the gas, and we follow the tracks into the woods.

"Go slow, and if we see any buildings, cut the lights immediately," Gray orders, suddenly sitting erect, gun in hand.

James nods in acknowledgment and guides the SUV forward through the snow. It's twenty minutes of pure agony as we drive down the road, all of us on high alert. That's when we see it looming ahead of us in the darkness. The cement building fills the vehicle's front window, blocking what light there is from the moon.

James stops the vehicle immediately, and we all sit for a moment. There aren't any cars or lights that we can see. The warehouse appears to be abandoned entirely. The only signs of life are the two sets of tire tracks that lead up to the building.

"We'll move in just like we did at the last place. I'll take the lead. James is second, and Kee, you bring up the rear. Everyone, keep your eyes and ears open. We have no idea what we're in for." Gray looks each of us in the eyes, and we nod and get out of the SUV.

The crisp early morning air cools the sweat dotting my body under my armor and gear. I take a deep breath, calming my heart and nerves as we move down the road toward the building.

*Please let us find something.*

We approach from the side of the building under the cover of the nearby forest and shadows. Moving along the edge of the structure, Gray looks through the windows.

Gray crouches down and motions for us to join them before we enter the building. "I don't see any lights, and it doesn't look like anyone is in there, but let's be prepared either way."

Gray stands before the door and motions for James to open it. I take up position behind James to swing around and follow Gray into the warehouse as another set of eyes.

James opens the door. Gray moves forward, sweeping left as I sweep right. It's almost colder in the warehouse than it is outside. James follows us both in taking point as we collapse around him and move silently through the space.

In the middle of the darkened room is a chair and table. The rest of the place is eerily empty. We walk toward the center of the room, sweeping constantly from left to right.

As we approach the chair, I stumble as I see the pool of congealed blood on the tabletop. I catch myself and come to a stop next to Gray and James.

"It doesn't mean anything, Kee." James' voice is barely a whisper, yet it still seems to bounce off the walls of the abandoned warehouse.

We move closer to the chair and table and can now see the chains hanging from the rafters, and the batteries, the knives, and all of the tools that Kiera must have used on Marcus still in the place where they were last touched.

Panic begins to edge into my mind as I look at the torture scene before me. Was Marcus able to withstand what she did to him?

"James, please take some photos of the scene, just in case there's something we can use here," Gray whispers while still sweeping the room. James opens the top left pocket on his kit, pulls out a camera, and starts taking photos with it, moving forward for a better angle.

I stay where I am, vaguely aware of what's happening around me and that I must pull myself together.

"Kee? Kee … I need you to stay focused," Gray whispers.

I look down at the gun in my hand that's hanging limply by my side and try to snap myself out of it.

I pull my heavy arms up and use my rifle to ground me in the moment and situation.

"I'm good," I whisper back, even though nothing about me is fine right now.

James finishes with the photos, and we move through the rest of the warehouse to see if there's anything else that might be useful in finding where Marcus is.

After we've secured the building, it's clear that nothing else there might help us out, and we start back to the SUV. Leaving the cold, dark, cement building behind, we move back into the night, walking along the tree line just in case someone is watching.

We ride in silence for the rest of the trip back to the safe house. My worry for Marcus grows with every passing moment. I hate that I can't do anything for him, that I don't know where he is, and that we're essentially searching blindly for him.

The air is thick with silence as we drive through suburban Moscow's empty, darkened streets. It's too early for anyone to be out yet, and it seems like we are the only ones that exist in the world right now. We see a few lights through the windows of early risers, but no soul in Moscow knows what we know.

My heart might be breaking.

I'm trying to keep it together, but the silence makes my heart heavier.

"He'll be fine, Kee. I know it." Gray's voice cuts through the silence and startles me from the growing panic spreading from my chest through the rest of my body.

"I hope so. We need to find him soon, Gray. I'm getting a bad feeling." Fear makes my voice hoarse, but I can do nothing to mask it.

Gray turns in their seat to look at me. "Trust me, I want

to find him just as badly as you do. Marcus isn't just my partner, he's my family. I'll do anything to find him. I need you to know that."

Looking into Gray's eyes, I can see how serious they are. I know that they mean every word that they're saying.

Nodding, I give a weak smile and sit back, trying to relax for the rest of the drive.

Before I know it, we're pulling up to the old, brick, two-story townhouse we've set up in. The rest of the neighborhood is dark except for the two front windows of our house. Hannah and Luke must still be up waiting for us to get back.

"I'll brief Luke and Hannah. Why don't the two of you try to get some rest," Gray says as we all step out of the vehicle and walk to the front of the townhouse.

Gray stops me before I walk through the door. "I know it's hard and scary, Kee, but I need you to be strong and focused so that you're ready to do what needs to be done when the time comes. I need you to be on top of your game."

"I understand. You have nothing to worry about. My sole focus is ensuring we get Marcus back safe and sound."

# CHAPTER 20

## Marcus

Voices rise and fall from the connecting room as I lay in bed, still covered by a mountain of blankets.

I feel better, solid, and like I can sit up without too much effort if I try. I have no idea how long I've been asleep, but I feel … good. I feel more like myself than I have in a while.

Moving slowly, I start to remove some of the covers so that I can ease myself up. The air in the room smells like the wood-burning fireplace in the corner and a bit like pine.

I drag my body up into a sitting position, careful not to use my hand that's been heavily bandaged. I can see the fingers poking out of the tops of the bandage and can, to my relief, move them without too much pain. The spike that Kiera drove through my hand must have missed the most important things. It hurts like hell, but it's a good sign that I can still feel and move my fingers. At worst, I likely broke some of the bones, and I can handle that.

The bullet wound in my leg, and the gash on my side have both been cleaned and are heavily bandaged. There doesn't seem to be much blood or seeping from the wounds, which I take as a good sign.

Now that I'm sitting, I can see from the window at the foot of the bed. All I see are bare bones, trees, and snow. There's nothing outside that would suggest we are close to civilization. Wherever I am is as remote as where Kiera was holding me. This does little to bring me any comfort. I would kill to be in the city right now, with access to, I don't know, a taxi or some way to get the fuck out of here.

The voices in the other room get louder. They're arguing over what they should do with me. The man's voice rises as he tries to convince the woman that they should turn me over to the police, and the woman argues to take me to the hospital. I don't like either of those options.

I don't know where Gray would be if they came here to help me, and I have no way of contacting them either. So, that leaves me with only a few options: the hospital or the U.S. Embassy. We can skip the police.

Wincing from the pain in my ribs, I slowly swing my feet over the edge of the small bed. The floor is fucking frigid, and I pull my bare feet back under the warmth and safety of the covers as soon as they touch the icy wooden floor.

Looking around, I see new clothes on the chair next to the dresser. Looks like I'll have to brave the cold floor to get dressed. Wrapping one of the blankets around my shoulders to cover my bare chest, I manage to stand slowly and put some weight on my injured leg. I hobble over to the chair and quickly grab the stack of clothing before limping back to the bed. Just that short walk took a lot of effort, and I'm winded.

I must be in worse shape than I thought.

Surprisingly, the clothes fit me pretty well, and the wool socks start bringing warmth back to my chilled toes as soon as I pull them on. Every small move I make takes a mountain of energy I don't have.

Taking a deep breath, I stand up and start toward the door, only to have it swing open before I can reach it.

"You're up!" the woman exclaims, taking several hurried steps back into the arms of the man standing behind her.

"Sorry, I didn't mean to scare you. My fucking bladder is about to explode. I just got up and need to use the restroom … toilet?" I point to the small room, hoping they understand enough of what I'm saying to get the point.

Nodding, they both step to the side, and I slowly limp toward the bathroom to relieve myself.

While washing my hands, I look into the small mirror above the sink. I don't even look like me. My short, salt-and-peppered hair is unkempt, greasy, and sticking up in every direction. My beard is wild, and the bags and bruises under my eyes make me look sunken and ill.

Cupping my hands, I splash the warm water on my face and run my hands through my hair. Leaning down, I position my mouth under the faucet and slurp.

I'm thirsty and hungry, but it's almost an afterthought. My body has too many things to worry about to realize my hunger fully.

Emerging from the bathroom, I find the couple sitting at the small dining room table, whispering to each other.

I give an awkward wave. "Hi, I'm Marcus. Thank you for taking care of me. You saved my life." I walk forward slowly with my good hand reaching to shake their hands.

They're cautious, but the man eventually stands and offers his hand to me. I shake it, and then the woman, his wife, gives me her hand.

"We were worried you would die here," she says. "I'm Marta. This is my husband, Sasha. We are happy that you didn't die."

Her English is halting but pretty good, and I'm confident Marta understands me better than Sasha.

"Again, thank you for taking care of me. Did you find me close to here?"

"Sasha was out hunting and found you in the woods. You were not in a good way. You're fortunate he found you."

Nodding, I sit at the table, suddenly feeling shaky and weak.

"I'm sorry, but do you have something to drink or eat?"

"Of course!" Marta speaks to Sasha, and he heads into the kitchen, grabbing some jerky and a glass of water.

I've never been happier to see jerky and have to remind myself to eat it slowly, so I don't upset my stomach.

"Thank you," I mutter around a mouthful of jerky, washed down with water.

"Do you have a cell phone, or can you take me to Moscow? I have friends I can call that can meet me there."

They look at each other, and after whispering, Sasha reaches into his pocket and hands me his cell.

My hand shakes as I reach for it.

*Don't get your hopes up, Marcus. There's still the chance that Gray didn't get your message.*

Looking at the keypad, I type in Gray's number and pray that somehow, they're already in Moscow.

# CHAPTER 21

## Kee

We step through the front door and are greeted by the smell of fresh coffee and warmth. The whole place has a soft, warm glow. It would be a great tiny home if it wasn't outfitted to withstand war and utterly bare of personal touches. The space is the opposite of the two buildings we saw tonight. It's warm and inviting, not cold and full of hopelessness.

Luke and Hannah come around the corner when the door shuts and locks behind us.

Hannah rushes forward, falling into Gray's arms for a deep hug as James and I move around them toward the kitchen, each of us giving Luke a nod.

"Let's go to the kitchen for a debrief," Gray says, grabbing Hannah's hand. Luke follows and sits back down at the kitchen table where he has been working on his computer researching Kiera.

"What did y'all find?" he asks as he looks from the computer screen to our group.

"So, the warehouse was completely empty, but there were signs of a shootout. An area indicated a struggle, so they likely took Marcus alive and held him at the second location we found."

"Second location?" Luke asks.

"Yeah, another warehouse about fifteen minutes up the road from the original coordinates we got from Marcus' text. It was also empty, but there were signs of torture, so I'm fairly confident he was held there. It didn't seem like it had been empty for too long."

James steps forward with the camera and hands it to Luke, "Here are the photos I took. It also looked like the blood was congealed, but not fully, so I don't think we're too far behind them."

"So you think he's still alive?" Luke asks.

"I think so. I would guess they took him alive, and there's a high probability that she's interrogating him about Dimitri's case. Kiera will want information on her father's case to figure out how to help him, so I don't think she's one to dispose of Marcus too quickly. She'll try to use him in some way first."

"What are our next steps?" I ask, looking around the room.

"Luke, how's the research coming along? Anything of significance?" We all turn to look at Luke as he stops typing to look at each of us.

"We may have something, but I need to dig more. Kiera and her family own *a lot* of properties, and we're going through them to see which might be good places to hold someone, but it's taking us a while. Send me the coordinates to the warehouse you found, and I'll see if I can pull up some satellite images for the area. Maybe we can see where they went."

Just as Gray is about to speak, their phone starts to ring. Gray looks at the phone in confusion for a second before picking up.

"Gray, what is it?" Hannah asks, seeing the look of shock on Gray's face.

"It's … Marcus."

"What?! Where is he? Is he okay?" The questions start pouring out of me as soon as his name leaves Gray's lips.

"What? Wait, I can't hear you? Where are you? Luke, I need a pen and paper." Gray goes to the table and starts writing something down on the notepad next to Luke.

"Okay, we'll be there in like an hour. How are you?"

I reach for the phone, taking it from Gray's hands as they finish writing down the address that Marcus gave them.

"Marcus! Are you alright?" I try to keep my voice calm but can feel my whole body shaking as I hear his raspy voice over the phone.

"Hey there, I'm okay, promise. I'm looking forward to seeing you and getting the fuck out of this country."

"We're leaving now and will be there soon. Just hang on."

"See you soon, love." It's the first time he's called me anything besides my name, and I can't help but think that he must be in bad shape if he's calling me a pet name.

"Luke, I need you and Hannah to stay here. Hannah, I need you to set up a place to provide medical support. It sounds like he needs medical attention, so we need to be ready when we get him back to the house." Gray and James move toward the door, and I follow them out, giving Hannah a look that I hope reads as encouraging. I know she would prefer to come with us, but part of our job here is to keep her safe. She needs to stay in the safe house and out of Kiera's sight.

Getting into the vehicle, Gray turns to me. "It sounds like he's been through it. He wouldn't give me details, but I could tell by his voice that he was in pain. So we should be ready for that as we pull up. He didn't want to go into detail over the phone, but it sounds like he managed to escape from Kiera, and some locals found him and have been caring for him the last couple of days."

Gray puts their hand on my shoulder to comfort me. My heart feels like it will beat out of my chest, and my concern for Marcus is almost shocking in its intensity. I'm also conflicted at how much information Marcus gave Gray in such a short time. Why would he not share that with me when I asked him?

I sit back in the seat and try to catch my breath and get my wits about me. It's best to go in with a clear mind. I don't want to show up and overwhelm Marcus with my anxiety. I can be clinical about this. I need to compartmentalize my feelings for him and focus on getting him back, ensuring he's okay, and then I can lose it.

I fully intend to discuss with him that he just ghosted me and went on this little mission of his, all half-cocked. If he thought he would get away with pulling something like this, he has another thing coming. He's going to get a piece of my mind … right after I make sure he's okay.

I have no idea where we're going, but we're not in Moscow anymore. It's much more remote, with trees lining the road. We're near Bosco Zanet, the National Forest. We have transitioned from streets buffered by houses to a single lane with trees on either side. It feels like we're taking the backroads around Moscow and seeing a part of the area many don't visit or know exists.

"Where are we going?" I ask, watching the trees blur into a solid line as we speed by.

"The location Marcus gave us is a little petrol station near here. He said it's the closest thing to the people who helped him. I guess it was as far as they were willing to take him to get picked up."

"How far out are we now?"

"About thirty minutes," Luke says, looking at the navigation system.

"You alright?" Gray asks, looking at me over their shoulder from the front seat.

"Yeah, I'm okay. I'm ready to be there and get him back."

"Me too," Gray says, turning back and looking out the window.

"How long have the two of you known each other?" Luke asks Gray, trying to keep the vibe in the car light.

"Marcus and I have been partners for about five years, but we've known each other for eight. He was my trainer when I first started with the DEA. Then he went on special assignment for a year before we linked back up and started working on Club Midnight and Dimitri."

"What was he like as a trainer?" I ask, curious to learn more about the man who's captured my affection.

"Just like he is now, a complete idiot. But he knows his shit. He's caring but will let you know when you've fucked up." Chuckling, Gray looks back at me. "This one time, we were in pursuit of a suspect, and I took off after the guy, leaving Marcus behind, and I ended up getting shot. I thought Marcus was going to finish the job. He was so pissed! He made it clear that if I ever did something like that again, he would either ask to be assigned a different partner or recommend that they pull my badge."

"Yeah, that sounds like Marcus," I mutter. "I bet you have a lot of stories like that." A feeling pings through my stomach, and I'm unsure what to make of it. Am I jealous of the connection that Gray and Marcus have? They have all of this time together and know each other so well, and I'm only just starting to scrape the surface of who Marcus is.

"You have no idea. Between stories of him reprimanding me for doing my job and stories of what he does when he drinks too much, I've got some good ones!" Gray laughs, a full-bodied sound that carries through the entire SUV. It instantly puts me at ease. It's good to know that Marcus is a good partner and cares so much for Gray. It tells me what I think I already know, which is that Marcus is a good, kind, caring man.

I can't help but smile and chuckle along with Gray. "What about you, Luke? How long have you known Marcus?" I might as well lean into their sharing and try to get more information about Marcus' past since he doesn't share much.

"I only started working at Midnight about a year ago. That's when I met both Marcus and Gray. I always thought there was something else between you but never could quite put the pieces together. Finding out that you all were DEA agents made much more sense." The way Luke talks about Gray and Marcus makes the jealousy in my gut grow. Was there something more between them at some point?

I look from Luke to Gray and see Gray smiling and shaking their head at Luke's statements. "We get that a lot, but we're really close, that's all. Marcus has been there for me through some seriously traumatizing stuff, and vice versa. We've been through some heavy shit that's brought us close together. He's the family I've never had, and I think he sees me as a younger sibling that he's gotta watch out for." Gray's voice fades as we all grow silent, looking at the small building that appears in front of us.

There's a single car parked next to it.

I hold my breath as we pull up next to the car. Is Marcus in there?

I look to the side and try to see through the dirty window, but I can't see if anyone is in the vehicle.

"Stay in the car—"

Before Gray can finish telling me to stay in the car, I'm already opening the door and moving toward the old, dirty

LADA Granta. Gray moves behind me, and Luke soon follows.

Leaning in, I peer into the car.

It's empty.

"What that fuck, Gray? No one is here."

"Maybe we beat them?" Gray offers, looking around. The cold Russian air burns my lungs as I take a deep breath and look around the petrol station. There are no signs of anyone else having been here. The fresh snow in front of the building is undisturbed.

"Do you hear that?" Luke asks from near the front of the car.

Gray and I go still, straining to hear what Luke is hearing.

"Sounds like gunfire," he whispers.

"Can you tell the direction it's coming from?" Gray asks, looking around.

"Hard to tell," Luke says, closing his eyes and focusing as distant gunshots echo around us.

I've had enough of the guessing. Walking past Gray and Luke, I open the door to the front of the station.

"Are there any houses near here?" I ask the man behind the counter, who looks absolutely stunned by my appearance. I can't say I blame him. I'm in a tactical vest with an oversized black coat, and I probably look like a psychopath.

"A what?" he asks in broken English.

"A house, a … dom … house," I say, struggling to think of the right word in Russian.

"Ah, dom, yes. Two … two roads on the left." The man holds up two fingers and points down the road in the opposite direction that we came in from.

"Thank you, spasibo," I say, turning and running out of the building.

"There are two roads on the left. It's the second left.

According to the gas station owner, there's a house on that road," I say breathlessly, jogging up to Luke and Gray.

"Let's see if our boy Marcus is causing more trouble," Gray says, running around the front of our SUV and jumping in the passenger seat as I slide in the back and Luke gets behind the steering wheel.

Tension settles over the car as we mentally prepare for what will happen.

It's not long before we pass the first side road on the left. There are no signs of any vehicles having gone down that road recently.

"Keep your eyes peeled for the next turn," I say anxiously, looking out the window.

"There!" Gray points ahead of us, where the snow has been recently disturbed by a vehicle.

"Windows down. I want us to pull over and go in on foot as soon as you hear or see anything. "I want the element of surprise," Gray says as Luke slows to take the small dirt road.

"Copy," I say from the back seat as I check my Glock 19, holster it, and pick up my Colt M4 Carbine, ensuring it's operational.

I meet Luke's eyes in the rearview mirror and give him a nod to show my readiness.

Luke nudges the SUV forward, and we crawl down the road at a pace that kills me. I want us to drive faster to get there and help Marcus. I don't want to wait another minute.

"There. Pull over where that small clearing is next to the road, and we'll walk in from here. I'm looking at the GPS aerial photos, and a small house at the end of this road is not too far from here." Gray holds the phone up for us to look as Luke navigates the slushy, slick snow and parks the SUV just off the road.

Stepping out of the vehicle, I glance at Luke and Gray

for guidance. They're both far more experienced in these scenarios, and I expect Gray to take the lead and Luke to bring up the rear. Gray looks from Luke to me, and with a nod, we all fall in and start moving down the road just as I suspected we would.

It's not long before the gunfire becomes louder, and as we round the last bend in the road, a small wood cabin comes into view. The structure is getting absolutely demolished by the six men standing in front unloading their automatic weapon clips into it.

I can see the wood splintering and flying with every bullet that strikes the small, innocent-looking wooden building.

Gray motions for me to move to the opposite side of the road and for Luke to go to the right. Gray will take the middle, and when they give the signal, we will move as one and open fire on the men before us.

At least, that's what I think is going to happen. That is, until a Molotov cocktail comes soaring through the shattered front window of the house, exploding in front of the men firing at it.

"Come on, you fuckers!" Marcus' hoarse but venomous voice booms from the house as another flaming bottle comes flying.

"Fuck it, let's go!" Gray shouts.

# CHAPTER 22

## Marcus

Handing the phone back to Sasha, I take a deep breath and slump in the chair I'm sitting in. It's as if every bit of strength I had is suddenly gone. All the stress of not knowing how to get out of here and back to safety is gone now. I can finally relax. I lean forward, rest my head on my one goodish arm, and try to slow my heartbeat and breathing. I can't believe I got out of this alive.

"I'm fucking lucky," I whisper, looking at my wool-covered feet against the worn wooden floor.

I look up and give Marta and Sasha a weary smile. "My friends are on their way to get me. They should be here in maybe an hour or so." Marta smiles and comes around the table to refill my cup with hot coffee.

"I can't thank you both enough. Thank you very much, spasibo ogromnoe," I say around the sudden lump forming in my throat. Christ, don't let me cry now. I know it's because all the stress and tension is leaving my body, and I'm still probably in shock, but now is not the time to break down. Not yet. Once I return to the team, I can let myself feel a bit. Just a little.

Marta and Sasha help me get into a pair of his boots that are just a little too small to be comfortable, but they're better than nothing. A car door slams as I stand up to test them out.

I look at the clock on the wall. It's been about forty minutes since I called Gray. It's doubtful that the team is already here.

"Wait, we said to meet at the gas station," I mumble as my tired and battered brain struggles to catch up and put the pieces together.

"Do you have any weapons?" I look to Sasha, knowing he has at least the one he held on me earlier.

"Yes, a few rifles," Sasha says, already moving to grab them.

"Marta, we need to flip the table, and you need to go into one of the back rooms. I think it's about to get wild in here."

Marta grabs a few things and heads into the small back room, out of sight, while Sasha walks up, handing me a hunting rifle and a handful of shells.

I've barely loaded the rifle when the first round of gunfire erupts from outside, and bullets pelt the wood cabin.

"Fuck, get down!" Grabbing Sasha, I push him behind the table and follow more slowly, kneeling carefully behind the thick oak table and readying myself for what's about to happen. "You should run. Take Marta and run out the back. You have time to get away still," I say, looking at Sasha.

He shakes his head and, clutching the rifle close, looks over the top of the table, waiting for me to tell him what to do.

I don't know how many men are out there. Still, the gunfire is nonstop, ripping pieces out of the house, shattering the windows, and peppering the interior with debris.

Just as I'm about to run for the window to fire back, there's a tug on my shirt. Turning around, my eyes are filled with flames, and there's Marta, bless her. She's got a Molotov cocktail in each hand and a massive smile.

"I could kiss you, Marta," I say, reaching for the flaming liquor bottles. Taking one in my hand, I instruct Sasha to do the same, and we make our way to the window as there's a break in the gunfire raining down on the house.

Heaving the Molotov cocktail through the window, I shout the only thing that comes to mind, "Come on, you fuckers!" Having thrown mine, I motion for Sasha to toss his next, and then we both hurry back behind the tables as the gunfire starts again. Except this time, the gunfire isn't at us. Peeking around the table, I move toward the window and quickly look outside. The men shooting at us are now huddled against the vehicle as gunfire pelts the ground around them, kicking up snow and pinging against their SUV.

"Sasha, now!" I shout and start firing at the backs of the men who had us pinned down just moments ago. Sasha does the same, and soon, the men are scrambling for their vehicle, carrying two of their own who have been shot.

Their SUV screams out of the driveway, spitting dirt and dirty, slushy snow everywhere as gunfire follows them down the drive. From the shattered window, I peer out and see some of my favorite people. Gray, Luke, and best of all, Kee.

All the emotions and feelings hit me, almost bringing me to my knees. I don't think I've ever been happier to see someone in my entire life. The relief and pure exhaustion I experience when I see Kee makes me feel the impact of the last several days. Seeing her reminds me of what I would have been missing out on.

Kee is absolutely stunning in her tactical gear. Her braids are pulled into a ponytail, and her face looks strikingly fierce. Seeing her makes my heart stutter in a way I haven't experienced before, and it's all overwhelming as she steps forward, taking my face in her hands and kissing me. It's a kiss full of anger, hope, desperation, and perhaps want.

I've missed her and feared that I would never see her again, and I hope she can see that reflected in my eyes because I don't have the words to properly verbalize it to her.

# CHAPTER 23

## Kee

My breath catches in my throat as what's left of the front door swings open.

For a moment, I can't keep the tears from prickling my eyes. He doesn't look like the man I saw weeks ago. His hair is a fucking mess, he's got a beard, and I can tell he's in a tremendous amount of pain. He's hunched over as he struggles out of the cabin, and one of his hands is heavily bandaged. His face is shades of blue and black, and he looks exhausted.

I can't stop myself. I hand Luke my rifle as I break into a jog, and moments later, I'm holding his face in my hands, looking into his eyes. The one is so swollen he can barely open it, but I can glimpse the bloodshot blue eye under all that swelling.

"You fucking idiot." I didn't think those would be the words that would come out of my mouth first, but they are.

I kiss his chapped and swollen lips while trying to be gentle with his bruised and battered body.

"Hey, you," he says hoarsely. I've never heard his voice sound like this before. It's so gravelly, almost as if he's been screaming a lot.

The tears threaten to spill over as I look at him.

"Hey, you two, why don't you get in the car so we can get outta here," Gray calls from the driveway. I can see Luke jogging down the road to bring the SUV to us.

"Gray, do you mind showing my new friends some gratitude?" Marcus says as I drape his arm over my shoulders and help him walk from the cabin toward where Gray is waiting.

Gray quickly pats Marcus on the shoulder. "Good to see you, man. You had us worried."

"Trust me, I had myself worried too."

Gray smiles and continues to the porch of the cabin, flashing Sasha and Marta a smile before apologizing for how their home was destroyed and passing them a large wad of rubles.

Marcus turns, waving to them both as Luke brings the SUV to where we are standing. Gray turns and starts heading back to us, ready to get the hell out of this place.

Gray opens the door, and I gently help Marcus settle into the back seat. He's winded from the short walk between the cabin and the vehicle, making me worry more about his well-being.

"Are you alright?" I ask, pushing a mop of hair off of his clammy forehead.

"I will be. I need some time," he says, wincing and settling into the seat.

Closing the door, I hustle around the back of the vehicle and get in on the other side. I want to be close to him, but I suspect he's got broken ribs, and the last thing he needs is someone bumping him as we head down the road.

"Hannah's here, so she can look at you once we get back to the house." I place my hand gently on his thigh and am surprised when he jerks it away, his breath stuttering.

"Sorry ... you surprised me." He looks sheepish at having jumped, but his exhaustion wins out as he lays his head back against the seat. "Sorry," he whispers again, looking at me. "Did you say that Hannah was here?"

"Yeah, she insisted on coming. The whole team is here."

Gray gets back into the vehicle and turns to look at us both.

"You look like shit, old man," Gray says, smirking at Marcus.

"Thanks, I feel like shit, and old," Marcus says.

"Let's get you back to the safe house."

"Sounds wonderful." With a sigh, Marcus leans his head back again and, to my surprise, reaches for my hand.

I let him take it, watching as he threads our fingers together.

"I was worried I wasn't going to see you again," he whispers so softly that I almost don't hear him.

"You don't need to worry about that anymore."

His eyes close, and he leans into me and falls asleep before we even pull away from the cabin.

Marcus' head rests on my shoulder as we drive back to the safe house. He's entirely out of it and exhausted. The ride is not smooth, and the fact that he doesn't flinch or complain about the bumps is worrisome, to say the least.

I'm still shocked that we were able to find him and bring him home. It doesn't make sense that he was able to get ahold of us and that he happened to be found by a couple that wouldn't just turn him over to the authorities. We really lucked out.

As we round the corner to the block that our house is on, I gently squeeze Marcus' hand in an attempt to wake him. He stirs slightly but doesn't fully wake up. With my other hand, I gently caress his unshaven and bruised face and whisper his name softly.

"Marcus, wake up. We're here."

My gentle approach has the opposite effect that I was

hoping it would. He violently jerks awake, pulling away quickly and pushing himself back against the door. His shoulders sag, and he grabs his side, wincing in pain. Looking like a caged animal, I can see the fear in his eyes before he realizes he's safe and not with Kiera.

I reach for him but stop myself. I'm afraid to touch him. I don't know what Kiera did to him, but touching might be a trigger.

"Are you alright?"

Nodding, he settles back into the seat with a wince and a sigh. "Sorry, I don't know what happened."

"It's okay. You've been through a lot in the last couple of days. Take your time, Marcus. We're in no rush."

He nods again and looks out the window. "Where are we?"

"Pulling up to the safe house now, we'll move you and Kee inside and ditch the vehicle a few blocks away. Hannah and James are waiting for you inside," Gray answers from the front seat. Their brow furrows in concern, seeing Marcus' response to my touch.

Gray has first-hand knowledge of what Kiera is capable of, and I can see the questions, concerns, and fears running through their head and reflected in their eyes. We must be thinking the same thing.

What did she do to him?

The more I think about it, the more enraged I become, and by the time we pull up to the house, I'm ready to explode. When I find that bitch, I'm going to make sure she knows she shouldn't have fucked with us.

I'll make her regret every mark that she put on his body. That's a guarantee.

Pulling up to the safe house, I get out with Gray, and we help Marcus exit the back seat. We let him take his time, as it's clear that he's in a lot of pain and is in worse shape than we may have initially thought. Once he's out of the SUV,

Luke drives off to park it, and we help Marcus up the steps. One at a time, letting him rest when he needs it.

It takes us several minutes to climb the ten steps to the front door, and he's winded when we get there, leaning heavily on Gray and me.

Gray enters the security code, and the door opens to Hannah coming down the hall, ready to help us move Marcus to the room she's set up as a makeshift ER.

"Hey Marcus, how are we doing?" Hannah is fully prepared and ready to help Marcus when we walk in. She's in full doctor mode, from the smile on her face to the shoes she's wearing. I'm overcome with gratitude and am so happy she fought to come with us.

"Let's get you settled and have a look at you," Hannah says, taking Marcus' arm from Gray and helping me move him down the hall.

The back room of the house has been converted into an examination room. Hannah has used one of the dressers to lay out the instruments she may need and has everything ready.

Hannah and I help Marcus onto the bed, and I turn to Hannah to brief her.

"It's okay, Kee. I'll take it from here. I'll let Marcus tell me what happened." Hannah doesn't ask me to step out; she's telling me to, and even though I want to stay with him, I know it's best if I do as she says.

I hesitate, looking from Hannah to Marcus, before turning to Marcus and gently taking his hand. "I'll be right outside."

Marcus nods and closes his eyes as he leans his head back. Hannah reaches for me and gently guides me from the room.

"I'll take good care of him, Kee, and will let you know if I need help. Let the rest of the team know that we're not to be bothered unless I call for someone, okay?" Hannah uses her soft doctor's voice, and I understand precisely why they use that tone. I'm comforted and calm and fully confident in what she's doing.

"Okay, but don't hesitate to call if you need help." I slowly back out of the room, looking at Marcus one last time before turning and heading toward the kitchen.

# CHAPTER 24

## Marcus

I feel like I'm dreaming. I can hear Hannah and see her, but it doesn't seem real.

Maybe I'm finally going into shock now that I'm back with the team. Perhaps this is my body coming off the adrenaline and survival mode. Maybe.

I'm exhausted. It's almost impossible to keep my eyes open, even as Hannah asks me questions and tells me to stay awake.

I hear my own voice talking but am not aware of doing it.

I know I'm here, but I feel disconnected from my body, drifting in and out.

Consciousness comes floating in.

I'm aware of the smell first, me. I smell, and it's not pleasant. I need a bath so badly. The second thing I notice is how good I feel. There's an underlying sense of pain, but it's not overwhelming. I'm not in tremendous pain like I was before. I'm … comfortable. I'm warm and don't feel like I'm dying.

I haven't opened my eyes yet. There's a part of me that's scared too. What if I wake up and I'm back in the warehouse? What if it was all a dream and none of it actually happened? What if I'm back with Kiera?

Taking a breath, I open my eyes. Well, I try to. I can't seem to open one of them—it is too swollen, or maybe something is covering it. I open my one eye and hold my breath as I look around.

I'm in a bedroom that looks like it's been converted into a clinic. Everything is sterile and clean, and it even smells like a hospital. I'm on a bed, covered to my chin. The door is closed, and I can hear the faintest sounds of voices coming from somewhere on the other side.

I want to move but have the same fear about moving as I did about waking up. I don't want to feel the pain I felt before. I'm not ready for that and just want to enjoy this feeling without the stabbing pain for a few more moments.

Turning slightly, I see a glass of water on the small bedside table. It's so close yet far away, and I'm thirsty. I'm tempted to break the moment's serenity to reach for the water when the door to the bedroom opens.

Hannah walks in, looking every bit at the doctor that she is.

"Oh! You're awake! That's great. How are you feeling?" She closes the door behind her and walks toward the bed while pulling a chair up.

I nod toward the water, unsure if my voice will even work.

"Of course! Sorry." She brings the water to me and helps me take a few small sips. Just enough to wet my mouth and throat. The water is room temperature, and I can feel it traveling through my parched body, hydrating as it goes.

"How are you feeling?" Hannah asks, putting the water back on the bedside table.

"Okay, I think," I manage around the sore throat.

"I'd like to take your temperature and check your bandages. Is that alright?" Her voice has a pitch I've never heard before, making me study her closely with my one good eye. She looks tired and a bit worn, but there's warmth coming off her in waves. Waves of caring, I realize. I swallow hard and nod my agreement.

"Let's take this patch off your eye first. I put it on there to let your eye rest and to keep it covered just in case any of the wounds around it opened again. I had to open a few areas around the eye to help reduce the swelling. It will probably be blurry for a few minutes but should clear up once I put the drops in."

It's just as she said it would be as she takes the dressing off my eye. I blink several times, trying to lubricate it and get the blurriness to disappear, but it doesn't help.

"Here come the drops." The blurriness seems less now, but it's still there. I close my eyes and let the drops sit for a few minutes before I try again.

Running a digital thermometer across my forehead, Hannah furrows her brow and writes something down on her clipboard.

"You've got a slight fever, which normally I wouldn't worry about, but given what you've been through and the number of injuries you have, I'm worried that you've got an infection somewhere, so we need to keep a close eye on your injuries and start you on some more antibiotics." It's like she's almost talking to herself, but I nod anyway.

"Alright, I'm going to pull the covers down and look at your injuries, starting with your ribs, and then I'll look over the gash you have on your side, your gunshot wound, and the various cuts and burns to ensure they're healing and that nothing looks red or swollen."

"Are you ready?" she asks.

"Ready," I rasp out as she grasps the top of the blankets and begins pulling them down.

I don't know what I expected but seeing my body like this hits me hard. I look skinnier than anticipated, and I am covered in various bruises. My ribs are the worst. They're black and purple in the center, with varying greens, blues, and red colors radiating out in every direction.

"You're fortunate," Hannah says softly, gently probing the area around the bruise. "You broke several ribs but managed to avoid a collapsed lung. Given the severity of the breaks, it's rare not to see a punctured lung or other internal injuries."

"Everything here looks good. Now, let's look at your hand."

"My hand?" I look down at my right hand, having somehow forgotten what happened.

"Again, you're pretty lucky. The stake broke some of the bones in your hand, but you have mobility in your fingers and wrist, so they're reparable. I stabilized everything the best I could, but you'll need surgery in a week or two, once the swelling has gone down, to ensure everything heals properly. If you don't have the surgery, you'll lose the use of the hand over time."

"Surgery?" I say, feeling the pull of sleep even as I'm talking.

I must have slurred my words because Hannah looks up and gives me a soft smile.

"I think that's enough for today. I'm going to change your IV bag and add more antibiotics. Do you want more water?"

I nod, and Hannah helps me take a few bigger sips than before.

I lay back, feeling exhausted just from this little bit of interaction.

"Kee? Is she okay?" I mumble, trying desperately to keep my eyes open.

"Yes, she's outside. I'll let her know that you asked about her. Do you want her to come in?"

"Not yet," I whisper. I want to be more aware and more awake for Kee. I don't want her to see me like this.

My mind becomes foggy, and I feel the effects of morphine dulling my senses, making my body heavy, and soothing my pains. It's a sensation I'm familiar with from injuries sustained in the past while on the job. I look to Hannah.

"I just gave you a little to help with the pain. It should help you sleep as well. You're still weak and need more rest. Sorry I didn't tell you before pushing the morphine."

I give her a nod, and before I turn my head back, I'm already slipping under. The bedroom fades around me as darkness creeps in from the sides, and I drift back into nothingness.

# CHAPTER 25

## Kee

Hannah walks into the kitchen, beaming.

"Is he okay? Is he awake?" Hannah has been checking in on Marcus every couple of hours, and this is the first time she's come out with a report like this one. This time it's different. My heart stops when she comes out of the room, shaking her head.

"He's awake."

"That's good, though, that he's finally awake?" I ask.

"Yeah, it's a good sign that he was awake and coherent. I am also a bit worried about his eye. The swelling has gone down, but he's still having trouble seeing out of it. We'll have to watch it closely to ensure it doesn't worsen."

Nodding, I look around the kitchen. We've all been sleeping in shifts, and it's mine and Luke's turn to be on watch. I'm glad that I'm awake to hear the news about Marcus.

"Can I go in and see him?"

"Not yet. He said he needed more time, and I just gave him morphine, so he's already asleep. You'll probably be able to see him in the morning if he's up to it." Hannah gives me a knowing smile, touches my arm lightly, and starts walking toward the stairs.

"I'm going to get some sleep. Wake me up if you or Marcus need anything."

"Will do," I say, sitting across from Luke, who hasn't looked up from his computer since Hannah came into the room.

"What are you working on?" I ask, leaning forward, elbows on the tabletop. I thought since we found Marcus, Luke and the team he's working with would stop what they were doing.

"Research."

"Right, not a man of many words, I guess," I mutter, leaning back in the chair.

My comment gets Luke's attention, and he looks up, pushing a pair of glasses up his nose. I hadn't noticed the glasses before, and they give him a bookish look that is entirely at odds with his body and personality.

"The team is investigating one of the other properties we identified as part of Kiera's holdings. They're trying to rule it out as a location where she may be hiding. I'm watching their progress on the drone footage."

Moving around the table, I sit next to him and look at the computer, where a small grainy image can be seen. It's an infrared image of six figures moving through a forested area. Their warm bodies stand out starkly against the color of the cold snow.

"Are these guys military?" I ask, watching them work in formation.

"Former. They all used to serve in one branch or another and now work for the same security firm. It's the same one that I work for now." Luke seems to straighten as he talks, and it's clear he's proud to be a part of their organization.

"Do they only work for private clientele, or do they work for the government sometimes as well?"

"Mostly for private clientele, but they are asked to do some stuff off the books for the government every now and then. I don't think that happens very often, though." He's glued to the screen, watching the team move from the trees to the building.

Before I can ask another question, the screen lights up.

"They've got contact." I can't hear what's going on, but I can see the team returning fire and moving to infiltrate the building as they do. "They're getting shot at!" Luke sits up straighter in his chair and grabs the headset from the table.

They breach the front and back doors of the building and move as one unit toward the middle of the room where the gunfire seems to be coming from. One of the figures goes down on the screen, and I see Luke tense. Whatever he hears over the radio isn't good.

"Get Hannah." He glances at me briefly, worry making his blue eyes cloud.

"Right." I hurry to the stairs, taking them two at a time, reaching Gray and Hannah's door in seconds. I knock once and then open the door. Hannah is already getting dressed and looking concerned.

"One of the team members who's going after Kiera got hurt. Luke's on the radio with them now."

Gray opens the door wider, pulling a shirt on. "Go wake up James. We may need him."

I nod and run down the hall to the last door. I raise my hand to knock, but the door swings open.

James doesn't say anything. Having heard us in the hallway, he nods at me and moves quickly with me down the hall.

We all rush down the stairs to our makeshift comms room, where Luke works with the team to evacuate.

"Hannah, I've got the team medic, Neko, on the line." Luke passes the headset to Hannah as soon as she enters the room.

"Go for Hannah." She naturally takes over the situation, advising the medic through stopping the bleeding and clamping the artery that was hit. It's intense, and we're all waiting impatiently to be of some use.

"What's your ETA? Right, we will be ready for you." Hannah hands the headset back to Luke and turns to the rest of us.

"The team will be here in about twenty minutes. We need to find a space for the injured."

"You can put him in my room." Marcus' voice is soft and a bit slurred. He has managed to get himself out of bed, IV pole and all, and is standing in the kitchen doorway in his boxers with a blanket over his shoulders.

"What the fuck are you doing out of bed?" Gray demands, walking toward him.

"You guys were so loud. How could I not be out of bed?" Marcus responds. He's clinging to the doorframe, and I can see it's taking a ton of effort to stay upright.

Hannah and Gray rush over to him, turn him around, and head into the living room between them. I hang back, unsure if Marcus will want to see me. What if he doesn't want me near him?

Following behind them, I catch Marcus' eye as they turn him around to put him on the couch, and he gives me a warm smile. Or at least as much of one as he can at this time. Putting my self-doubt aside, I help Gray and Hannah set Marcus up on the couch so they can focus on the incoming trauma.

"Gray, help me in the back room. We'll need to switch out the sheets and get it ready." Hannah says, grabbing Gray's arm and leading her out of the room. I hear them jogging to the end of the hall as they hurry to turn the room around in time for the injured team member.

It's just Marcus and me now. He's lying on the couch, eyes closed, breathing heavily from the exertion.

"Are you just going to stand there?" His whisper is barely audible, yet it's the loudest thing in the room besides the beating of my heart that I swear he can hear.

He opens his eyes, blinking at me before holding out a hand.

I'm moving before his hand is fully raised. I don't need anything else. I rush forward and settle on the edge of the couch, taking his palm in mine, careful not to touch or bump his injuries. I perch lightly on the edge of the sofa.

"You had me worried for a bit," I whisper.

"Had myself scared." He tries to give me a smile, but it falls short, and I see naked vulnerability on his face.

I want to reassure, kiss, and make him feel better, but I'm scared to touch him too much. I'm afraid I'll hurt him or give him flashbacks of what Kiera did. Even as I think this, I find my hands lightly feathering over his injuries, as if my touch can take away some of his pain. I gently caress his face and let the feeling of his beard tickle my fingers. I can't keep my eyes off him as he lies on the couch, caught between a morphine dream and reality.

"Are you feeling okay? Is this okay?" I ask as I caress his face before gently pushing his hair back and running my hands through it. I start to run my hands through his hair over and over again in a soothing rhythm.

"Yes, this is fine. It feels nice," Marcus whispers with a slight groan that reminds me of the sounds he makes in bed.

I chuckle softly. "You're such a big baby."

He graces me with a smile and soft chuckle that crinkles the skin around his eyes. One of my favorite things about him. My hand runs through his hair, and my eyes run over his body. All of the wounds, the pain he must have experienced, it makes me tear up.

"No tears, Kee. I'm alright," Marcus whispers, taking my right hand in his as I gently cup his face with my left.

"You really scared me, Marcus. You left without saying goodbye. What if I never got to see you again? What if you had been killed?" I'm searching his eyes, his face, desperately looking for something to tell me he regrets what he's done. Something that shows that he feels for me what I'm feeling for him.

"I know. It was reckless. I wasn't thinking about how it would impact you. I was overcome with the need to get revenge for what the Ruez family had done. I was wrong, Kee. I know that." He kisses my palm gently.

"Can I … can I kiss you?" I ask tentatively, not wanting to rush him.

"I would like nothing more."

Leaning in, I brush my lips against his chapped ones and kiss him slowly. Pulling back, I reach for his face again and gently run my thumb along his cheekbone.

He leans into my touch and closes his eyes.

"If you ever do anything like this again. I'll kill you myself. Understand?"

"Never again," he agrees and leans into my hand more. I kiss him again, wanting to be as close to him as possible.

I want nothing more than to curl up on the couch with Marcus and to feel his arms around me again. The time we've had together has been too brief, and whatever is growing between us is just getting started. We need more time together, and I want to take full advantage of his being stuck on the couch.

"I'd like to lay with you on the couch if that's alright, or I can stay here if it will be too painful." I don't want to push him too far and give him an out in case it's too much for him to handle right now.

"I'd like that." Marcus goes to shift when the front door flies open, and a flurry of large men dressed in black surges into the small space of our safe house.

I watch as they spill into the room and know that Hannah will need help dealing with the chaos. Glancing from the door to Marcus, I give him a small smile, but before I can say anything. He takes my hand, squeezes it, and kisses it gently.

"Go, go help," Marcus says, nodding his head toward the chaos in the hallway.

"I'll be back as soon as I can."

Getting up from the couch, I jump into the fray, looking to Hannah to tell me what she needs help with. I don't know their names or anything about the team, but one of them was injured trying to help us, so we owe it to them to help.

Luke guides the two men carrying the injured man into the back room where Hannah is waiting. I can see blood on his face by his mouth, which looks terrible. Wherever he was hit, it looks like some damage was done.

"Alright, put him down on the bed." Hannah motions for the two men to put her patient on the bed where Marcus was.

"Who's the medic?" Hannah looks around from large man to large man until someone steps forward. "You? Good, you stay. The rest of you need to leave the room so we can focus. If we need you, we'll let you know."

"Right, guys, you heard her. Everyone out. They've got this!" I shout from behind, trying to usher them out of the small space. "They need room to work." That seems to be effective, and the group starts to file out.

They're all massive guys. Very clearly military or former military, most over six feet tall and well-muscled. They fill the small space of the hallway with their bodies, which are only made larger by their kits.

"Guys, let's move to the kitchen and clear out this space a bit," I say, gesturing for them to move down the hall.

"Fuck, fuck!" One of them hisses as they move down the hall. I can see in their faces that they're worried for their teammate. I can tell they're a tight-knit group, and the rest likely take it personally when someone on the team gets hurt.

"Does anyone else need medical assistance?" I ask, glancing quickly over the rest of the men.

"We're all good," says a tall man with a shock of gray shooting through the front of his midnight-black hair.

"Kee, Gray, James, this is the Feather Flight team. Neko is the medic. He's in the room with Hannah right now. The guy that got shot is Finn. This guy here is Mika." He gestures toward the tall man next to him.

The rest of the team introduce themselves as John, Dalton, and Eric. They're a mixed group of guys in age. Mika and John are the more experienced in the group, and Dalton and Eric are the younger ones, along with Luke. I didn't get a good look at Finn or Neko, but I'm guessing they're of similar age and build as the rest of the team.

"What happened out there?" I ask, setting the freshly brewed coffee on the table along with a pitcher of water for them.

"It was quiet as we approached, and there weren't any indicators of hostiles in the building. They seemingly came out of nowhere and caught Finn as we were ready to breach. I should have been more careful. We've done so many of these buildings that I think I got complacent." Mika runs a hand wearily through his hair.

We can all see his worry and exhaustion by how he's standing, and the lines on his face.

"Why don't y'all sit here or in the living room with Marcus and get some rest. We have rooms upstairs if anyone needs to crash for a while," Gray says.

"Thanks. We'll crash here and wait to hear what Neko and the Doc say about Finn." Mika pulls out a chair as he talks and sits down at the table.

"Did you see anything, by chance, that would indicate what Kiera's plans are?" I ask, looking at Mika.

"No, but I think it would make sense for Kiera to return to the States. From our intel and surveillance, maybe she's done collecting her men and gear here in Russia."

"Have you heard anything or seen anything that might indicate that?" John asks, speaking for the first time as he leans against the wall, arms crossed over his chest. He's built like a brick house, his dark skin and bald head shining in the kitchen light as he settles against the wall.

"No, we haven't heard any chatter from Kiera or her men since we arrived," Luke responds, sitting again in front of the computer he's been monitoring. Putting his glasses back on, he looks at the laptop as if it will tell him at any moment that Kiera is on the move.

"Do we have alerts for facial recognition or anything like that?" I ask, walking over to where Luke is sitting and settling behind him next to Mika.

"Yeah, but we haven't had any luck. No pings or anything, so I'm not sure if she's using a good disguise or flying private, so we don't have access to those cameras and airports." Luke looks from me to Mika. "Sorry guys, I've done what I can here."

Gray gives Luke a tight grin. "You've done great, Luke. Let's keep an eye on things for a little longer, and if all else fails, once Finn and Marcus are given the okay, we'll plan on heading back home."

Mika nods in agreement, and we all settle into the room,

ready to wait until we hear from Neko or Hannah about the state of their teammate.

The room falls into a comfortable silence, only punctured by coffee cups being set down and the occasional scuffing of boots. Their team looks exhausted, and it would do them good to rest, but I know no matter how much I recommend they sleep, they won't until they know how Finn is.

Glancing into the living room, I can see Marcus is out cold. Gray comes up beside me, placing a comforting hand on my shoulder. "He's going to be okay, Kee. He's been through a lot and always comes out on the other side."

"What do you mean he's been through a lot? What has happened to him?" I ask, looking at Gray.

"Let's just say his ex-wife left him when he was struggling. She couldn't handle him being on the force and dipped out. He just woke up one day and she was gone."

"When was this?"

"Years ago, I knew him before he was with the DEA. He used to be a cop, and things started going downhill when he got promoted to detective. Then, he got shot on the job, and it was while he was in the hospital that she left him. He didn't take it well."

"She left him while he was still recovering?" I look back at the broken man asleep on the couch and feel a tugging in my sternum. How could she do that?

"Yeah, left while he was in surgery and never came back. Having a spouse in this type of job isn't for everyone. I don't think he blames her. I think he's a little cautious about getting into anything serious because of work."

"I understand that. Thank you for telling me this. I won't bring it up unless he does." I give Gray another smile and head into the living room where Marcus is. Pulling up a chair beside the couch, I sit and take his uninjured hand in mine. I stroke it lightly while leaning over him to brush the hair off his forehead. He mumbles something in his sleep but doesn't wake.

Lost in my thoughts, I overlook Neko, who's standing at the crossroads of the living spaces. That is, until he clears his throat, stepping into the kitchen with his back to me. I remove my hand from Marcus' and stand near him to hear the updates.

His short, dark hair is standing straight up, and his gear is splattered with blood, as are his arms and neck.

"We managed to stop the bleeding and remove the bullet. He's fucking lucky, but the bullet did shatter his collarbone, and Doc says he'll need surgery." Neko sighs upon finishing the report, his shoulders falling as the tension leaves his body.

Neko is slighter than the others and Asian American, his olive skin paler than usual, given the circumstances. Luke comforts the other man as the adrenaline from the day's events wanes.

I watch as Luke hugs the more petite man and can't help but look to James, who's been quietly standing in the corner through the entire evening. He's watching the interaction closely, but his face betrays nothing. He's completely closed off.

"Well done, Neko. Finn probably wouldn't have made it if you hadn't been with us," Mika says, going to shake the medic's hand.

"Just doing my job, Mika," Neko says, shaking his head as Mika claps him on the back. "I'm going to get cleaned up, but Doc should be out soon with the full report." Neko nods to us and disappears down the hall toward the small restroom.

The news makes the air noticeably lighter, and we all smile, knowing that Finn will be alright. We need to get him back to the States now so that he can fully recover. We also need to get Marcus back soon so he can get his hand looked at by specialists.

Turning around, I head back into the living room to my vigil in the chair next to the couch. Marcus hasn't moved since falling back asleep. Even in sleep, I can see the laugh lines on his face. It's hard to believe that someone so … light, has been through such hard and trying things. I place his hand in mine again and trace small circles with my thumb on the back of his in a soothing motion.

I can't wait to get him home and healthy, so I can kick his ass for putting us through this.

# CHAPTER 26

## Marcus

My entire body hurts, and I'm fucking miserable as I settle into the seat of the cargo plane.

"You know you can lie down, right?" Gray asks, looking at me and pointing to the extra stretcher on the deck.

"Fuck that. I'll sit." I hate flying, and the last thing I want to do is lie down on the fucking deck of the plane. I'd rather sit and be fully strapped in.

Gray chuckles and sits between Hannah and the other stretcher.

Finn is his name, and he got shot because of me. He almost died because of me. I feel tremendous guilt over his injury and that it's so severe. Injuries like his are hard to recover from, and it will take time to rehabilitate from them. I hope the kid can recover and still be on the team.

I'll have to chat with him once he's up and on his feet; thank him for what he did for looking for Kiera.

I look away, letting the shame wash over me, and close my eyes, unable to make eye contact with any of the other members of Finn's team.

"You alright?" Kee asks. Out of the corner of my eye, I see her place her hand on my thigh before catching herself and clasping her hands in her lap. I appreciate the effort she's going through to make sure I'm comfortable. I'm okay with small touches, but when someone makes contact with me without knowing it's coming, I'm immediately back in that chair, strapped down, with Kiera's hands roaming over my body. I want to be okay, and I want Kee to be comfortable and not have to watch herself around me. I reach out, take her hand in mine, and place it on my thigh, holding tightly to her hand.

"Yeah, just ready to get home." My tight smile does nothing to reassure her, and she reaches over, brushing my hair off my forehead.

It's something she's started doing here in Russia since I was injured, and I find it calming to lean into her touch. I still get flashes of Kiera on my body—her hands, her nails scraping down my face and chest—but being around Kee helps. She calms and anchors me.

Kee leans over, resting her head on my shoulder. "We'll be home soon, and then we can try to figure out how to put all this behind us."

"I missed you … while I was gone. I thought about you a lot." I don't know why I say it, but it comes out as I look down at her. Her full lashes flutter against her beautiful dark skin.

"Mmmmhmmm, you should have thought of that before you went off on a solo mission like an idiot," she mutters, not looking up at me.

Guilt washes over me again. I've made a mess of everything and am having difficulty knowing I've caused Kee and the Flight team so much grief. "I'm sorry, but I didn't feel like we had other options. And then I learned about Dimitri being involved with my dad's death, and I had to do something."

"Wait … Dimitri was involved with your dad's death? I didn't know this. Gray mentioned that you found something that had to do with your family. I didn't realize it had to do with your dad. I'm sorry, Marcus."

"Yeah, they matched the ballistics from some of the weapons at the club with the bullets from the shooting where my dad was killed. It's been Dimitri this whole time. He's the one who's responsible for everything." I look down and realize that I'm gripping Kee's hand hard. Taking a breath, I try to relax and loosen my grip.

"We will get him, Marcus. I promise."

"I know we will." I feel the warmth and heaviness of the painkillers Hannah gave me seeping through my body as we start to take off. I let them begin to tug me into oblivion. I lay my head on Kee's, allowing myself to fall into nothingness.

# CHAPTER 27

## Kee

The bump of the plane landing on the tarmac wakes me up. My neck is sore from resting it on Marcus' shoulder. The flight back seems to go faster and soon we're preparing for landing. As we taxi down the runway, I glance over at Marcus. His salt-and-pepper hair is unruly, and his once-tanned skin is now pale against the bruises that smear across his flesh. I brush the hair off his forehead before I can stop myself, and he jerks awake with a small gasp. Looking around wildly, he calms immediately when he realizes where he is and sees me. His grip loosens on my hand as he settles.

"Sorry, I didn't mean to surprise you." I rest my free hand on his forearm, feeling the tension leave his body as he settles back into his seat.

"It's fine. I must have been really out of it. I don't remember much of the flight. Are we here already?"

"Already?" I jokingly ask him. "For those without painkillers, it was a grueling eleven-hour flight!" I give a small smile, hoping my humor will settle him more. It works, and he returns my grin, wincing as his swollen face resists the movement.

The plane stops, and we gather our belongings and prepare to disembark. As the cargo door opens, I'm surprised to see a couple of SUVs waiting for us, along with an ambulance.

"Who arranged all of this?" Marcus asks as Gray walks up to stand beside us. "Luke's friends, the Feather team. Impressive, right?" Marcus nods, and Gray and I help him stand up until he gets his feet under him.

"The ambulance will take you and Finn to the hospital where Hannah works, and the rest of us will follow in the SUVs," Gray says before they walk away to help Hannah and the rest of the team move Finn's gurney.

"Are you feeling any better?" I ask as I walk slowly with Marcus out of the plane and toward the ambulance.

"I feel fine. I don't think I need to go to the hospital."

I can't help but roll my eyes. "Ugh, what is it with you and Gray and hospitals?" I nudge his shoulder softly, and he chuckles with me. I use my humor to lighten the mood and avoid the more serious things that I don't want to think about just yet, like the fact that Marcus still has a fever, that he hasn't moved the fingers on his injured hand in a while, and the fact that we still don't know where Kiera is. I feel a tingle move through my body as my anxiety ramps up.

I'm worried about Finn as well. He hasn't woken up yet, and Hannah's concerned about that. It will be good to get both of them checked out.

I help Marcus into the ambulance, and the team loads Finn in. "I'll be behind you in the SUV," I say as the doors close.

Gray, Hannah, and I jump into one of the SUVs with Luke and Mika. The drive to the hospital takes about thirty minutes, and the vehicle is eerily quiet. All I can think about is how Marcus will recover from this. His body and mind took a hell of a beating, and I'm worried that one will heal and the other will get pushed to the side. I don't think this trauma will be one that quickly goes away for him.

"Pull into the ambulance bay. They're waiting for us there," Hannah directs Gray. Getting out of the SUV, we help Marcus and Finn get loaded onto their stretchers.

"I can walk. I don't need a stretcher," Marcus says as he starts toward the door of the ER.

"Get on the damn stretcher," I say, giving him a challenging look and crossing my arms over my chest. Marcus looks at me, surprisingly giving up the fight and slowly settling onto the stretcher.

"Wait ... wait ... did Marucs just listen to you without a smart-ass comment back?" Gray says, looking between the two of us.

"Damn straight he did. See, you can teach an old dog new tricks." I beam at Gray and Marcus as we push the stretcher toward the door.

"I'm not that old," Marcus says as we enter the hospital.

"Aw, keep telling yourself that, boo." I give his hand a light squeeze to show that I'm joking with him, and we stop at the front desk where Hannah's friend and fellow doctor Cassie is waiting.

"I'm glad you all made it back in mostly one piece!" Cassie says, smiling at all of us. I notice that her eyes linger on Finn and the Feather team's medic, Neko, before sweeping across the rest of the group. I follow her gaze and realize that we must be making quite a scene with how we look.

We've all changed into civilian clothing, but you can't overlook a group of 6-foot-something muscle men in a hospital with two injured people, especially when one has been shot. I catch a few of the other doctors and nurses glancing our way.

"Let's get you all checked out. I'll be taking Finn back with me, and Marcus, you have a date with Dr.

Brimingham." Cassie picks up two charts, keeping one and laying the other at the foot of Marcus' stretcher. As they move Marcus, I look at Hannah and Gray.

"I'll be going with Marcus unless the two of you need me for anything." I give James a nod as I walk past. He'll take primary care of making sure Hannah is looked after while I'm with Marcus.

We still have to be on the watch for Kiera. We have no idea what she's up to or where she is. For all we know, she could be planning a hit on Hannah, Gray, or even Marcus.

I know that Luke and his team are still looking into it, but at this point, anything is possible.

We near a room toward the end of the hall, and an older man in a white coat steps out, directing the gurney into the room. I go to step in, and the man stops me. "Sorry, but if you're not family, you can't come in. You are more than welcome to wait here, though." Nodding, I settle in the chair next to the door to his room.

The weight of the last couple of weeks is starting to weigh on me. I feel the fatigue settling in and know the crash will follow soon. I don't have time to let that happen. Kiera is still out there. I'm sure she knows that Marcus escaped by now. I don't know Kiera well, but she seems like the type to go after someone simply because they managed to get away. I don't think we've seen the last of her, and I'm sure she'll be taking some shots at the rest of us. There's no time for any of us to let our guard down. Not yet.

I'm so focused and lost in my thoughts that I don't notice Mika and the rest of Luke's teammates settling in the seats around me. Finn must have been taken to a nearby room. Looking around the hallway, it seems like something out of a movie. Large bodies consume every ounce of space, imposing and suffocating. Yet they offer nothing but safety for those they protect. I'm glad that they're on our side, fighting with us.

The vibrating of my phone makes me look down. It's a message from James.

> I've secured Gray and Hannah at the townhouse and will stay with them until we know more about Kiera and our next steps. Please keep us updated on Marcus and Finn.

Typing out a quick response, I look around the hallway again. Taking in the faces of each of the men risking their lives for our group. Making eye contact with Mika, I give him a smile and a nod, which he returns. I can see the weariness in the set of his face and in his eyes. We all need a break. I hope we wrap this up quickly and get back to normal. Whatever that is.

The doctor steps out of Marcus' room, looking surprised at the number of bodies in the hall.

"Who's here with Marcus Wyatt?"

Standing, I walk to the doctor. "I am, I'm his … his … significant other." I fumble over the words, unsure what exactly we are and how I should label our relationship. They won't tell me anything if I don't play it right.

"I'm not going to lie. He has a long road ahead of him. We've got him on an IV to rehydrate and will take him up for surgery on his hand. His wounds seem to be healing well, and the electrocution has no long-lasting effects, at least not that we can tell right now. We will keep an eye on his heart rate and monitor it throughout his time here just to be sure. I would also recommend that he get a stress test to ensure his heart is in good shape. We often see issues with palpitations after injuries such as his."

I take in all the doctor's information, nodding along with him. My stomach flips every time he mentions something else that might be wrong or needs to be checked out. My palms are sweating, and I've got a funny feeling in the pit of my stomach. As Dr. Birmingham finishes his explanation, he smiles gently at me, touching my shoulder.

"Overall, he's fortunate. But he's not out of the woods yet and needs to keep his stress levels down. I've put in a call to the cardiologist so that they can come and do a more thorough examination before we operate. Do you have any questions?"

"Could I … see him before you take him upstairs?" I ask tentatively. "Of course, just keep it brief."

Nodding, I step around him and into Marcus' room. The nurses quickly remove themselves and shut the door behind them to give us a bit of privacy.

"They're taking you up for surgery soon," I say as I approach the bed. Marcus has been stripped of his clothes and is in a hospital gown that looks a couple of sizes too small for his larger body. They've left it pulled down so that his chest is exposed, and several wires are attached to his bruised and battered torso.

I sit gingerly on the edge of the bed and let my head fall forward until our foreheads are resting against each other.

"Are you alright?" Marcus softly asks, bringing his hand up to gently stroke my back. He lets it rest on my hip, and I'm immediately reminded of how he gripped that same spot not so gently when we were together.

"Am I alright? Shouldn't I be asking you that?" I whisper softly. I caress his bearded face carefully to avoid the more swollen and bruised areas. I pull away and look at his body. Fully taking him in for what feels like the first time.

His chest and stomach are mottled with shades of red, blue, green, and black. The large gash on his side has a fresh bandage on it that is already soiled with fresh blood. His hand is unbandaged but immobilized by a splint, and I can see the damage done to it. Tears prickle the corners of my eyes as I look at his broken, beautiful body.

"Kee …" A whispered prayer.

"Baby … I'm okay, I promise." His voice is barely above a whisper as he looks at me. His grip on my hip tightens before he pulls me closer for a half hug. "You promise you're going to be okay?" I whisper into his neck.

"Promise."

I lift my head, and our lips meet, finding each other as if connected by an unseen force. It's a soft kiss meant to comfort and reassure and does the damn job.

"Thank you," I breathe out for the first time in the last two weeks.

"Anytime, babe." Marcus gives me a little smile, and I lean into him more, finding comfort in how solid he feels. He may be bruised and look terrible, but the man is sturdy, and the feel of him against my body gives me the reassurance I need.

The soft knock on the door pushes us apart, and the nurse says, "We're ready to take Mr. Wyatt upstairs for the rest of his examination and to start prepping him for surgery." Nodding, I ease off the edge of the bed and move to the side so they can move him.

"I'll see you on the other side," he says, reaching out his hand.

I grip it quickly before they wheel him away. Giving him a reassuring smile and a small wave as he disappears down the hallway.

I slump back down in my chair, and Neko puts a hand on my shoulder. "Sounds like Marcus is going to be just fine."

"Physically, probably after some work. Mentally, what

I'm worried about. Kiera did things to him that would scar anyone, and he hasn't talked about it with anyone yet. I'm worried the longer it goes, the worse it'll get for him." I look at Neko, thinking I've put too much on him and that he'll be like most "tough guys" and overlook the effects of the trauma.

"I know a really great therapist that specializes in trauma and PTSD. I'll give her a call and set something up for him. I keep her on call for all of my guys," Neko says, giving me a knowing smile.

"Really? That would be great. Of course, Marcus may not like it, but I think he will need the support and someone to talk to who's a third party."

"Yeah, I'll take care of it and let you bring it up to Marcus. Just mention it and then give him some time and space to come around to the idea. It might take him longer than you want, but he's gotta process everything at his own pace."

# CHAPTER 28

## Marcus

Kee walks into my room, and I forget what I was thinking. She's got her braids piled on top of her head and is wearing a pair of skin-tight dark denim jeans and a long-sleeved black shirt that hugs her body, showing off her athletic, lithe build.

She's fucking stunning.

"How are you feeling today?" Kee asks, sitting on the edge of my bed.

"I'm ready to get the fuck outta here." I can't hide how irritated I am by the whole situation. I've been in the hospital for over a week and am so done with it.

"The doctors said you should stay here one more day, and then you should be good to go."

"Why are you in such a good mood?"

"It's Finn. He's been out of it since we brought him in. He went into surgery the other day, and he finally woke up!"

"That's a relief." I lean back in the bed and let go of the tension I was holding onto.

"So, I can leave tomorrow?"

"According to the docs, you should be good to go

tomorrow," Kee says, reaching up and swiping hair off my forehead. I follow her hand with mine, swiping at my unruly hair before running my hand over my beard. I can't wait to get out of here. I still haven't shaved, and my facial hair is unruly.

I want to feel like myself again.

"I'll be right back," Kee says, getting up and moving toward the door.

"Wait, you're leaving me already? You just got here!" I shout after her.

I'm beginning to think Kee isn't coming back when she walks in with a bag from the store down the street and a small bowl she got from god only knows where.

"What the hell are you up to?" I ask, trying to sit up straighter in my bed. I try not to wince as the stitches in my side and hand pull at the movement. I've got a few other stitches scattered across my body, and every now and then, I'll move just right to pull them too tight.

I breathe out once I get myself settled.

"I'm going to cut your hair and give you a shave," Kee says, coming out of the bathroom with a razor.

"The hell you are!" I look at her in feigned horror as she stalks toward me. "Look, I get out tomorrow. Let's not make any rash decisions."

Laughing, Kee sits on the bed beside me and starts setting up her station. Out of the bag, she pulls a travel-sized shaving cream, a pair of scissors, and the razor she had in her hand. Kee lays them all out on the small bedside table. She returns from the bathroom with a dish of hot water and a hot washcloth.

Maybe this won't be so bad.

Looking at her setup, she goes to the bathroom again and returns with a towel, "Okay, lean forward, old man, and let's get this hair under control." I do as I'm told, thinking how great it will feel to have her hands run through my hair.

"Are you good with sitting up like this?" Standing beside me, Kee asks, "How do you feel about moving to the bathroom? It would be better to do it in there."

At this point, I would do anything she wanted me to. "That's a smart move. Let's go to the bathroom."

Smiling to herself, Kee helps me out of the bed and into the bathroom. I can move by myself, but I like having her close to me, and I will milk it for all it's worth.

"Sit," she demands as she disappears to gather her tools.

I close my eyes as she puts the hot rag on my face and cuts my hair. I've got my head against the edge of the sink and try not to cringe whenever I hear and feel the scissors snipping away. The sound of metal against metal brings back memories of knives and chains I don't want to deal with right now.

I take an unsteady breath and focus on the proximity of Kee's body to mine. I can feel the warmth coming off of her and try to focus on that. On the feel of her thigh against my arm as she leans over me. The sensation of her long fingers deftly running through my hair.

"Head up," she whispers, and it takes me a moment to register what she's said.

Bringing my head up, she cuts the back of my hair, leaning close to me. The hot towel slips off my face, and I'm almost eye-to-eye with her as she cuts the strands above my ear.

"Hey," I say softly.

"Hey," she whispers back, giving me a sly smile before leaning in and pressing a soft peck to my lips.

"I could get used to this," I whisper back. I feel small breaths of air on my cheek as she chuckles at me.

"Wait until you see your hair before you say that."

"Oh no, what did you do to me?"

Full belly laughter erupts from Kee, and I'm suddenly scared to turn around and look in the mirror.

"Don't look yet! We're not done." Pulling up a stool, Kee settles between my knees and sprays shaving cream into her hand. Reaching up, she maintains eye contact and spreads it across my face. She picks up the razor. The glint of the light off the blade startles me, and I lean back, away from her. Kee looks from me to the razor, and realization flashes across her face.

Lowering the razor, she takes my hand. "You can trust me, Marcus. I won't hurt you. I promise. Do you trust me?"

Looking into her eyes, I can see her heart there, and I see nothing but warmth and something else that I can't express. Safety, maybe. Understanding? Love?

"Yes, I trust you," I whisper, feeling some of the tension in my chest lessen.

"I'll go slow, and if you need me to stop, just let me know, and I'll stop. We can go as slow as you need me to."

I nod, and Kee lifts the razor to my face, making the first pass. The feel of the blade against my skin sends shivers through my entire body, and I close my eyes. My hand grabs her wrist involuntarily.

"Sorry, sorry. I'm sorry," I say over and over again.

"Marcus. Open your eyes."

I do as Kee asks. There are tears in her eyes, but she's smiling at me.

"I said we would go as slow as you needed to, and I meant it. But I need you to know that if we stop, your beard will look really weird." She smiles at me.

I let out a tight little laugh followed by a deep breath.

"Okay, I'm ready."

She lifts the razor and makes another pass, pauses, and then another. Before I know it, Kee has shaved my entire beard. She takes the now cold wash cloth and runs it under hot water before applying it to my lower face.

"A whole new man," she says, leaning in and kissing my warm lips as she removes the washcloth. I glance at myself in the mirror as she helps me stand.

"Holy shit." I don't even recognize myself. I haven't been this clean-shaven in a long time and look about ten years younger.

"We almost look the same age now," Kee says jokingly.

"Damn you," I whisper, holding on to her tighter and going in for another kiss.

I kiss her deeply, letting my mind go blank for the briefest of moments and just enjoying the feel of Kee. I nip lightly at her bottom lip and feel myself starting to react to our kiss. She notices as well.

"Easy, old man. I'm not sure if you're up for that yet." She glances down and raises an eyebrow.

"I think otherwise," I say, going in for another kiss.

Kee laughs and dodges out of the way, knowing that I can't keep up with her. "That's unfair," I say, putting a slight pout in my voice.

"Get your ass back in bed," Kee says, winking at me.

Climbing into the hospital bed, I feel the familiar sense of exhaustion creeping in.

"Hey, I know you want to get out of here and get back to work, and you will, but it doesn't hurt to be a little cautious. Which I know is not one of your strong suits," Kee suddenly says as she walks over to the bed and helps me get comfortable.

She's not wrong. Look at where it got me this last time. In a fucking hospital with one working hand.

I hate to admit to Kee that she's right, but I don't have to. She knows she's right, and she knows that I know it.

I chuckle and shake my head. Kee is great at calling me out on my shit, which is precisely what I need.

"Come here," I whisper softly, holding my arm up for her. Kee instantly moves to my side and snuggles in. "We're getting good at this whole cuddling-in-hospital-beds thing," I say, pulling her closer to me as she settles in.

"Let's not get any better at it, okay?" Kee responds, laying her hand on my chest and looking at me.

"Deal," I say, kissing her full lips.

"Umm … sorry to interrupt, but I got a call from Gray." Luke stands at the door looking awkward but with his trademark goofy-ass smile.

"Don't you know how to knock?" Kee goes to sit up, but I hold her in place.

"The door was open!" Luke exclaims as if that's a good enough excuse.

"Shut it and get in here. What did Gray have to say?"

Luke walks into the room and sits in Kee's chair.

"So, according to Gray, there's been some whispering amongst the DEA that Kiera will try to break Dimitri out of custody. He's due in court next week, so they're beefing up security in case there's any truth to the rumor."

"Would she be dumb enough to try something like that?" I mutter more to myself than to anyone in the room.

"Please, you and I both know that she's dumb enough and desperate enough to do whatever she can to get Dimitri out," Luke says, leaning back in his chair and eyeballing me.

"Does Gray have a plan?" Kee asks, sitting up to perch on the edge of the bed. I keep our fingers locked as she moves away from me.

"Gray will try to get on Dimitri's detail if they allow it. But other than that, we're waiting to see what Kiera will do. What are your thoughts on it?" Glancing between us, Luke crosses his arms over his chest and waits to hear our ideas on countering whatever wild-ass plan Kiera has thought up.

"Why don't we try to get ahead of her and track Kiera down before she can make a move?" Kee suggests, glancing between us.

"We've been trying to track her down, as have the DEA, and we can't seem to get a read on where she is." Luke sighs, running his hand through his wavy blond hair.

I lay my head back on the pillow, feeling tired yet wired simultaneously. My mind is racing, and I can't stop thinking about how we need to catch Kiera before she does more damage. I hate that I can't do more, that I'm stuck in this hospital bed and am not out there helping the Feather team track down Kiera and her men. I've never been unable to do my job before. Yes, I've been hurt and out of commission, but I could still move and was still active in the investigations. This is different. It feels different. I don't feel like myself, and I'm not sure I'll ever be the same again.

"We need to get everyone together to review our options and see what the group thinks is the best move." I'm staring at the ceiling as I talk about the options we could propose to them. "Maybe we can convince the DEA to take a different approach to transport and handle Dimitri. I doubt they'll be open to our recommendations, though."

"Luke, let's pull everyone together tomorrow afternoon and get to work on a plan. The sooner we have something solid in mind, the better." I look at Luke, who nods his agreement and gets up.

"Sounds good. I'll see the two of you tomorrow. Take it easy with him, Kee. He's still recovering." A wink and a smirk follow Luke as he leaves the room.

If I was one to blush, I think I would be, but I've been teased enough in my day that I've got pretty thick skin. Kee picks up an extra pillow nearby and launches it at the back of Luke's head as he walks out. It hits the door with a soft thump before sliding to the cold hospital floor.

"Don't worry. You don't have to take it easy on me." With what I hope is a devilish grin, I reach for Kee to pull her close again. The look in her eyes causes me to pause. It's a mix of confusion and concern.

"Or do take it easy on me?" I say, looking at her for signs of what's running through her brain. I don't understand why she has that look, and I can't tell what she's thinking.

"What's going on in there?" I ask, tightening my grip on her hand.

"He's not wrong. You are healing and need to take it easy. I don't want you to push yourself too hard. We have a good team. It's not just you. You know that, right?" Her grip tightens on mine. It's beginning to make sense now.

"Are you worried about me?" I ask, trying to lighten the mood with some gentle ribbing.

"Yes, Marcus. I am worried about you. I have been worried about you and continue to worry about you. Please get that. I need you to understand that you're important to me and the others, that we care about you, and that you can't run off to do stupid shit like you did!"

Kee is standing now as she speaks, and her voice has risen incrementally in volume. I'm reminded of many of the arguments my ex-wife and I had that started similarly. A lump forms in my throat, and my stomach flips as the nerves ripple.

"Are you angry with me?"

"Yes! Yes, Marcus! I am angry with you. I'm pissed that you did something stupid and didn't think you could tell anyone where or what you were doing except for Gray. I hate that you put yourself in danger like that. What were you thinking?"

"That Kiera needed to be stopped. Someone needed to stop her."

"That someone didn't have to be you, by yourself."

"I realize that now. I know it was stupid and a bad choice, Kee. I was so focused on tracking Kiera down and stopping her that I didn't think about what would happen when I found her. It was dumb. It was really dumb. I know that." I hold out my hand to her again in the hopes that she'll come back to me.

Kee hesitates but then reaches out and takes my hand, allowing me to pull her into the bed again.

"I'm sorry, Kee, for being so reckless. I won't be doing anything like this again, promise," I say, gently kissing her lips, which she has set in a determined line.

"Don't placate me, Marcus. I need to know that you mean it. I need you to be safe just like you need me to be safe as well." She's looking at me with beautiful dark eyes, and something in my chest seems to break loose.

"I promise, Kee. I … am sorry, and I understand why you feel like this. I don't want you to think you aren't important to me. You matter to me, Kee. You matter a lot to me, and I don't want to lose you. I've had people leave me in the past because I've been reckless, and I don't want to push you to that point. I don't want you to leave me."

It's the most open I've been about my past in a long time and being vulnerable scares me to death.

"I'm not going to leave you, Marcus. I'm not like people you've been with in the past. You're special to me. You're my person. I just need you not to be so reckless. My heart can't take it."

"I can do less reckless," I say with a smile as I pull Kee in for another kiss.

# CHAPTER 29

## Kee

Leaving Marcus' hospital room gets harder and harder as the days pass. I wish I could spend every minute with him, but we've got to find Kiera, and it's all hands on deck.

Marcus doesn't know that we've also got security at the hospital. If it's not me, it's one of the guys from Luke's team. We've been switching on and off as the days have rolled by. There's no doubt in my mind that if Kiera finds out where Marcus is, she'll come for him, just like she'll likely make a move on Gray and Hannah.

Kiera is determined and demented. A dangerous combination. I've seen what she's done to the people around me and know she's capable of terrifying things. I hate that we're almost waiting to see what she'll do next. I've reached out to some of my contacts in the DEA and with the Marshals to see if anyone knows anything, and so far, all I've gotten back are crickets. Someone has to know something.

As I drive toward Hannah's, my mind keeps drifting back to Marcus and his promise to me. I know now isn't the time to make promises that can easily be broken, but I need him to see that he's not alone in this fight. He has a whole team fighting with him, and none of us will give up any time soon. I can't stand the idea of him going off on his own again to deal with Kiera. He barely survived this last time.

Pulling up to Hannah's townhouse, I wave to James as he sits in the car across the street. I know he's been pulling doubles to keep an eye on Hannah and Gray while I've been with Marcus. I need to get back to help him, but I want to ensure Marcus is safe.

I knock on the front door before letting myself in. Hannah's house has served as the temporary command post for our and Mika's teams. It means there's been a lot of people coming and going from the place. I'm sure James hates every moment, but it's a necessary evil.

I can't believe we haven't been able to get a lead on Kiera since she got back to the States. We know she's here. We need to find her before she moves to free Dimitri or takes out a team member.

Gray's convinced the DEA to let them work on the security detail for Dimitri, which is nice. They won't let Gray work in an official capacity, which is disappointing because it means she won't have the protection or authority of a DEA agent, which is understandable. She did quit, after all. Still, at least we have another set of boots on the ground while keeping an eye on Dimitri.

I walk into the sunroom at the back of the house and find Hannah with Luke. They're looking over information on one of his screens.

"Did you find something?"

They both look up from the computer screen.

"Maybe … I'm not sure yet," Luke says, turning back to the computer and pushing his black-rimmed glasses up on his nose. Somehow, the nerdy muscular thing works for him even though, in my mind, it shouldn't.

"I've got the team checking out a couple of leads that we got this morning. I'm hoping we will know more later this evening. It looks like some large explosives have been moved throughout the city lately. Everyone's buzzing over it, and all authorities are on high alert."

"That definitely sounds like Kiera. She would choose something big and distracting to get to Dimitri." I sigh as I sit on the couch across from Luke and Hannah.

"How's Marcus?" Hannah stands, crossing her arms over her chest and leaning against the arm of Luke's chair. They have become close, which is good since they've spent so much time together. Luke is essentially her second bodyguard now that I'm looking after Marcus.

"He's good, getting better by the day. More aware. They're sending him home tomorrow, so he should be arriving here once he's out."

"That's great! It will be good to have him in the house and help cut back on the hours everyone is spending on security. I know Gray will feel better having him here with us."

"Are we making a mistake putting everyone in one location?" I ask, looking from Luke to Hannah and back again.

"Strategically, it's not the best option. I can agree with you there. But I think it's our only option right now, given our manpower. We've got to make do with what we have," Luke says, looking up from the computer again.

"Once we know more about Kiera and her plans, hopefully, that will ease some of the tension, and we'll be able to set the team up in another location and perhaps move Marcus into a hotel or something. It's not ideal having you all here, that's for sure." Luke looks at Hannah and me before going back to his computer.

"I'm going to go switch out with James. I'm sure he's tired of being stuck in the car." I get up and pat Luke on the shoulder. I notice that he tenses a little at the mention of

James, and I hope nothing negative has happened between them. The last thing we need is for the two of them to not get along.

"Kee, wait!" Hannah follows after me as I leave the sunroom.

"What's up?"

"I'm worried about Gray going out with the DEA and not having protection. They don't want Gray to carry a weapon, and we had to fight them to get Gray a vest."

"I know it's been a struggle working with them. I can't even get anyone to give me the tiniest bit of information on what they think Kiera is planning. Everyone's being very tight-lipped about the whole situation."

"What can we do to keep everyone safe?" Hannah asks as she leans against the hallway wall.

"I think we're already doing it. We keep our eyes peeled, watch over everyone Kiera might try to attack, and monitor the situation. I know it doesn't seem like we're doing a lot, but it's all we can do now. I know it's frustrating."

Hannah agrees, "I know you're right, but I hate just sitting here waiting for something to happen. I feel like we need to be the ones to make the first move."

"I couldn't agree more. It's killing me just waiting around like this."

"You'll let me know if you figure anything out, right?"

"Absolutely."

"How are things with you and Marcus?" Hannah asks softly.

"Good, it's … good. He has a long road ahead of him and doesn't quite realize that yet, but he's progressing."

"That's great, but what about the two of you? How are things?"

"We're taking things slow, but it's good. We're still fig-uring each other out, I think."

Hannah gives me a knowing smile before turning around to go back to the sunroom.

I head to the front of the townhouse, passing by the rooms that were once empty but are now full of military-grade weapons and gear. It's weird looking around. The townhouse is the same, yet the contents have changed drastically. It's no longer the cold, empty place that it was. It's complete now.

Stepping outside, I head across the street to James.

"Ready to stretch your legs yet?" I ask, opening the passenger side door and stepping into the vehicle. James is not one to linger around for small talk, and our routine is that as soon as I sit down, he's out of the car. But not today. He stays in the driver's seat, looking down the quiet, empty street. It's just started snowing, and the weather has changed from late fall to early winter. Reminding us of our brief stint in the Russian winter not but a week ago.

"It's not so bad out here," he answers solemnly. He doesn't look at me; I know something is up from his demeanor. He's slouching slightly in the seat, another indicator that something is up. James is always professional, straight-backed, and on top of his game. Today, he's pale, with dark circles under his eyes, and he looks … rumpled.

"What's up? What's going on with you?" I reach over and place my hand on his shoulder.

"It's nothing." He won't look at me.

"Did something happen between you and Luke?"

"What would make you ask that? Why would that matter?"

I've known James for a long time, and if I push him, he'll shut down even more. I'll have to leave him alone, and when he's ready, he'll open up to me, or he'll get over whatever is bothering him.

"Okay, if you want to talk about anything, you can

talk to me. Anything at all, I'm here for you." I squeeze his bulky shoulder.

"The house can be a bit chaotic these days," he says softly, hands gripping the steering wheel.

"Yeah, there are a lot of people around. It's a good and a bad thing."

He nods, pausing before he opens the door. "How is Marcus doing?"

"He's good. He's getting out tomorrow and will be moving into the house."

"That's good. I'm happy for you, Kee. It's good that you guys have each other."

This gives me pause. It's rare for James to talk so much, *and* he just mentioned my relationship with Marcus, which is *really* weird.

"You're sure you're okay?" I reach for his shoulder again.

"Yeah, I'm just in a weird mood today. I haven't been sleeping much, been thinking about the past a lot lately."

"Let me know if you want to talk. I'm your partner and your friend, James. I'm here for you."

"Thanks, Kee. I appreciate it."

Getting out, I walk around the front of the car, shoo James out of the vehicle, and watch as he slowly walks across the street and into the townhouse. Hopefully, he will go home soon and get some rest.

I don't think I've ever seen him like this before.

Settling in, I turn the keys in the car and turn on the radio. I'm already counting the hours until I get to see Marcus again.

# CHAPTER 30

## Marcus

Hannah's house is a shit show. There are too many people here, and now I'm adding to the chaos. I'd kill to go back to my little apartment downtown and have some peace and quiet, but that's out of the question. Kee would kill me if I did that. I glance over at her as she closes the door behind us. She's got my prescriptions in one hand, and the other instinctively moves back to my arm to help me navigate the house.

As I walk down the hallway toward the sunroom with Kee, I'm greeted by several of Mika's men.

"Hey Marcus, how ya doing, man?" one of them asks. I haven't had a chance to learn all their names and have been too out of it because of the meds to remember those I've already met.

"Good, good. Just taking it one day at a time," I reply, giving the canned response has become second nature. If I was honest with myself and everyone around me, I think they should have kept me in the hospital longer. The truth is that I hurt everywhere and not just physically. My mind is so full all the time. It's … loud. I know it's anxiety, and

I usually can control it, but it's been running wild since Russia. Every loud noise, unexpected touch, and thought of Kiera makes me want to crawl out of my skin. I can't tell anyone about it, though. I don't want them to know I'm still struggling. I don't want to be a burden to them.

Kee helps me sit on one of the chairs in the sunroom, and I look around at the rest of the team that's already gathered there. Gray walks in behind us and stands next to Hannah, who looks up at them with a expression that makes me forget everything for a moment. You can see the love growing between them, but there's more than love in Hannah's eyes. There's trust.

"Alright, everyone, we've got a legit lead on Kiera, so it's time to buckle down and figure out how to catch up with her before she moves on Dimitri. We know they're planning to move Dimitri in a few days. Everyone is buzzing about the explosives that have been stolen recently and exchanging hands throughout the city." Gray jumps right into the debrief, and I try not to physically flinch every time they say Kiera's name.

"Luke, can you brief us?"

"Right"—Luke points to a makeshift screen rigged in the sunroom to project the operation details—"as Gray mentioned, explosives have changed hands in the last several days, and everything points to Kiera. Several sellers went to Midnight to make the drops, indicating Kiera's behind it. The part we don't know is the where and the how. We can assume that the attack will happen on Dimitri's transportation route from the prison to the courthouse. It's several miles to cover, and we've mapped out a few spots where we would set up an ambush if we were planning the attack."

"The plan will be to have two or three team members at each location during the transportation. We'll also start recon today to see if there's anything suspicious going on at those locations. I'll be with the transportation team handling Dimitri, so I'll have eyes on Dimitri and the immediate area. James and Luke will also be on the ground following the caravan and providing backup if needed," Gray says as they look down at Hannah and then up at me.

"Hannah and Marcus will be here, running comms and overwatch for the operation. Luke will walk you through what to watch for and any equipment you need to be updated on. Hannah's been shadowing Luke over the last week. Marcus has experience with this stuff, so I have full confidence in the two of you."

Gray continues to share the plan, but I'm not fully listening. It's a lot to take in just having come from the hospital, and my brain can't seem to wrap around everything Gray is saying. I know I'll be stuck in the house with Hannah, which I'm less thrilled about. I feel like I'm letting everyone down, like we're in this situation because I couldn't handle my shit in Russia.

Gray's voice cuts through my thoughts, "Alright, that's all for now. I'm off to chat with the DEA team leader. The rest of you have your assignments from Luke." There's a smattering of voices affirming what Gray has said, and everyone starts to wander out of the sunroom.

Kee moves next to me and drops her hand on my arm to help steady me as I stand up. They've set up a space for me in the dining room where I can rest but still be a part of the conversation. I glance at Kee's profile as she walks next to me. I don't look away fast enough, and she catches me looking at her.

"What's up?" Kee asks as we walk into the dining room.

"Nothing. Well, it's just … thank you. For everything."

Kee's grip on my arm tightens slightly before she runs her hand up my bicep and across my shoulders. Leaning in slowly, she kisses me on my freshly shaven cheek.

"You are very welcome." I'm blessed with a full-watt smile and can't help but smile back, the clouds in my head clearing briefly to take in her brilliance.

"You're stunning." I can't help but say what I think as I look at her.

I've caught her off guard momentarily, and Kee appears slightly flustered. I smile, feeling like my old self for a minute. It's as if all of this has been a bad dream for those few seconds of seeing Kee bask in my compliment.

Still smiling, she gives me a look I'm beginning to recognize and kisses me. It's soft and slow. She's taking her time. It doesn't matter that people are walking in and out of the room we are in, or that Kiera is still out there. Nothing matters now except for the feel of her lips on mine.

If I sit on this couch any longer, I might become a part of it. I've been here for hours, and my brain will not quiet down. The house is all but empty now, and the silence is deafening. It starts to settle in, and I feel myself losing it a bit. It's as if I'm back in that room, on that chair, with Kiera all over me. I'm sucked back there for a moment and can feel the pain again.

*Fuck.*

Running a hand over my face and swearing, I slowly get off the couch and return to the sunroom. I suppose it's better to be doing something than sitting and feeling sorry for myself.

"How's it going? Have they found anything?" I ask, walking into the room and standing near Hannah's shoulder.

"Hey! How are you feeling?" Hannah looks up from the screens in front of her and rubs her eyes as she focuses on me. She's been here for hours, and I'm sure she needs a break.

"I'm good. Do you need anything, maybe a new set of eyes?" I attempt to crack a joke and am rewarded with a quick smile from Hannah.

"Oh, Marcus, I feel like your dad jokes have gotten worse!" Hannah smiles again as I pull up a chair and slowly lower myself.

"What? Are you saying you're tired of my jokes?"

"Absolutely not. I don't know what I would do without them." Hannah's warm laughter fills the sunroom.

"But seriously, Marcus, how are you feeling? You doing okay?" Her green eyes are warm as she looks over at me.

"Yeah, I'm good, just a little frustrated. I feel like I'm holding everyone back and can't do anything."

"I assure you, you are not holding anything or anyone back, Marcus. We're doing everything we can to find Kiera before Dimitri is moved, and everything is going as planned, or at least as well as it can right now. Everyone worries about you and wants you to get better faster, so that's what you should focus on."

"Have they found anything?" I ask again, looking at the screens in front of Hannah.

"Everything looks normal, according to the team. They'll be out there all day. Kee will be coming back soon, though. Gray wants someone else to stay here with us just in case Kiera makes a move on the house." Hannah is starting to sound increasingly like she should be a member of Mika's team and less like a doctor with every passing day.

"That's probably a good idea since we don't know what Kiera is planning, and she's capable of anything at this point."

The front door opens, and Kee walks into the house, making her way to the sunroom, where she gives both of us a smile. "Look at you two, all cozy and shit. How's it going in here?"

"It's going well. Did you go to the courthouse with Gray and James?" Hannah responds while clicking something on the monitor in front of her. She's become adept at everything that's been thrown at her recently. It's truly impressive.

"I did. It all seemed normal. Gray and James will stay there longer to see if anything changes." Kee shifts toward me and places her hand on my shoulder.

I fight the urge to twitch or even jerk away from her touch. My skin feels raw. I know it's because of Kiera and thinking about what she did to me, but the feeling of someone touching me makes my skin crawl. I'm not mentally in a good place today, and every little touch and loud noise makes me jumpy.

I sit as still as possible but tense up. I know Kee can feel my muscles bunching under her hand, and I feel terrible about it. She's been great about dealing with me since we got back, but I know she'll get tired of babying me sooner or later. I need a little more time.

"You alright?" she whispers softly, leaning down. Her braids gently brush my shoulder and neck.

"Yeah, I'm okay." I give her a tight smile, and despite my best acting, she can read my face and removes her hand from my shoulder.

"Let's go get something to eat in the kitchen," she recommends, holding her hand out to me.

"Hannah, do you need anything?"

"No, I'm all good here. Take your time."

I stand slowly, letting my body acclimate to standing before stepping. I reach for Kee's hand and let her lead me to the kitchen.

"How are you really?" she asks as soon as we're out of earshot of Hannah.

"I'm fine … really. Just a little jumpy still." I lean against the counter and motion for her to come to me. I do okay if it's on my own terms and I know who's touching me. I can prepare myself for it, but when the touching comes out of nowhere, I can't help but flash back to the warehouse with Kiera.

"I think … I will need a little more time, but I'm trying," I say, feeling the need to explain myself to Kee. I don't want her to feel like I'm rejecting her or that I don't have feelings for her. I need her to wait for me.

"I understand. I want to be there for you, so let me know if I can do anything. Even if it means not touching you, tell me."

Do I tell her? I look at Kee and see, written across her face, how much she cares for me.

"Actually, if you could wait to touch me until I know it's you, like don't come up from behind me and touch me, that would be best. It freaks me out." I laugh it off a bit, but Kee isn't having it.

"You should have told me sooner. I would have kept my hands to myself."

"I don't want you to keep your hands to yourself. I need to see you before you touch me. That's all. I need to know for sure that it's you, Kee. If that makes sense."

"Completely." Kee steps into my open arms as I lean against the counter and motion to her. She's warm and smells of cocoa butter and fresh winter air. She carefully wraps her arms around my midsection to avoid the stitches on my side. I let my arms rest on her shoulders, pulling her in closer and letting her nestle between my neck and collarbone. She fits perfectly.

"Is this okay?" she whispers.

"Yes, this is perfect," I whisper back. Kee leans into me, putting more of her body on mine, and I lean forward, accepting it. Taking a deep breath, I lean into her and let my head rest against hers. The noise in my head stops, and all I can see, hear, smell, and feel is Kee.

"I missed you," I whisper, wishing I could pull her in closer than she already is.

"You've said that already," she jokes back.

"I mean it." Kee pulls back just far enough that our lips are inches apart.

"I want to kiss you," she says, looking at me for permission.

Nodding and leaning forward, I accept, and our lips brush tentatively before we deepen the kiss. Kee's lips are soft yet slightly chapped from outside in the cold. She tastes of peppermint and coffee, and I can't stop pulling her closer and deeper. She's perfect to me in every way, and I've been missing her kisses more than I could ever possibly explain.

The time away from her were some of the longest and hardest that I've ever experienced and have made me appreciate Kee so much more. The way she calls me on my shit keeps me in line, and she knows when to be delicate and soft with me versus being stern and the badass she is.

Our lips part, and I'm already wanting more. My hand cradles the back of her neck and the side of her face, pulling her in for another kiss. I'm not ready to be done yet, and neither is she. Her hands are roaming up and down my body, finally settling on my hips. She's lifted my shirt just slightly enough so that her fingers have found bare flesh. Her touch is electric and makes my heart race. If we don't stop now, I'm not sure we will be able to.

Now is not the time to be fucking in the kitchen, especially with Hannah just down the hall.

Not now.

I pull away, catching my breath and leaning my forehead against Kee's as we both try to get our wits about us.

"Later," I say, kissing her forehead, "we'll continue this later."

Kee chuckles and pushes into me. "Will we now?" She's grinning from ear to ear, and it's good to see. She looks like the Kee that I fell in love with months ago. Happy and carefree. Not burdened by what has happened.

I smirk at her, going in for another kiss, only to have her lean back and out of the way.

"Later," Kee says with a smirk and a wink as she walks out of the room.

# CHAPTER 31

## Kee

My heart is bound to beat its way out of my chest. Leaving the kitchen is the only way that I'll survive. Marcus' kisses have left me shaken to my core and utterly breathless. He feels new, different from before, and I can't figure out how or why. It's like we're meeting for the first time all over again.

His kisses seem … more meaningful than before. Like they meant something this time.

Holy shit.

I'm still trying to get my head straight when I walk back into the sunroom to check on Hannah and see how everyone is doing with their recon.

"Anything new?" I ask, sighing and sitting down next to Hannah.

I see her look at me out of the corner of my eye and do a double take.

"Are *you* okay?" she says, and I can hear the laughter in her voice.

"I have no idea what you could possibly be referring to." I'm smiling so hard that my cheeks start to hurt. "I am wonderful."

"Don't say a damn thing," I say, looking at Hannah.

"Nothing from me, I swear," she says, laughing and turning back to her computers.

"Ugh, damn him." I sigh again, crossing my arms and legs while leaning back in my chair.

"For real, though, anything from the team?"

"Nope, nothing. Everything seems to be normal. I think some of them are on their way back right now. Gray and James are still out at the courthouse doing a final sweep of the path they're planning on taking."

"I don't like this, not one bit. There are too many unknowns, and Kiera is far too unpredictable." I chew on my bottom lip as I fight the overwhelming worry gnawing at my gut.

"I agree. I don't like it, and I don't like that our people are out there with basically no protection and no way to fight back if Kiera does show up and try something." Hannah gives me a worried look, and I pull her into a half hug. Nothing about this feels right.

"It'll all work out, right? We've gotta stay positive and ensure that we're prepared for whatever the outcome may be."

"Right," Hannah whispers.

I know she's worried about Gray, and she should be. I would be terrified if Marcus was out there.

I get nervous before large operations, but this one is different. It's personal. Kiera has hurt so many people that I care about. I'm determined to help the team catch her. Even though it's been a while since I've been involved in any operation, I'm not letting my nerves or lack of experience stop me from helping the team.

The day is dreary and overcast. The courthouse is quiet now, but I know that will all change soon. It was big news when Dimitri got arrested, and it was revealed that he had been importing large amounts of drugs and weapons into the city. He's one of the major players, and his arrest sent waves through the criminal underground and the public.

I expect every reporter in town to be here when the DEA arrives with him. Everyone wants to peek at the monster turning our city into a playground for criminals.

James, Luke, Gray, and I are stationed at the courthouse while the rest of the team is spread out throughout the transportation route. So far, no one has reported anything. I've got an uneasy feeling about all of this, though, and I know that something is coming our way. I can't explain it, but a nagging sense of uneasiness has settled at the base of my spine, making me check my surroundings repeatedly.

I don't like it.

"Caravan has passed checkpoint two." Mika's voice in my ear heightens my focus on my surroundings. They're getting closer.

It's radio silence except for the teams checking in once the caravan has passed their locations. The feeling of unease tightens my stomach, and I look through the now-gathered crowd of reporters to the end of the block where I know James and Luke are. They're just a couple of blocks away now.

They're each on a corner, with James being the farthest away.

"Caravan has passed the final checkpoint, Gray. They're all yours." I glance at Gray from farther up the block where I'm positioned. They look prepared as they scan the surrounding area.

I prepare myself for the arrival and the chaos that will ensue. Dimitri is in the second car of the four-car transport, with security and support staff in the other vehicles.

The first car rounds the corner, then the second.

As the third SUV rounds the corner where James is, it swerves slightly before stopping about half a block from him. I see James and Luke start moving toward the vehicle, and dread hits me in the pit of my stomach.

"James and Luke do *not* approach the vehicle. I repeat, stay back at your posts!" Gray's shouts are ringing in my earpiece as the world explodes in a brilliantly violent flash of light and heat.

Even though I'm at the far end of the block, the vehicle's heat waves as it explodes send me and everyone around me flying. There are screams of surprise and pain as debris rains down around us. Vehicles three and four have erupted into flames. There's nothing but blackened asphalt, shattered windows, and echoing cries filling the air with the dark smoke rising from the scene.

My first thoughts are of James and Luke. They were both so close to the explosion. There's no doubt that they've been injured. My second thought is Dimitri and Gray. As I turn to look for the second car, all I see is the open door and the two dead DEA agents in the front and back seats.

Fuck, how? How did they manage this?

Finding a single person in the absolute carnage is impossible. Yet, I spot Gray picking themselves up from the blackened sidewalk around them. Gray isn't looking at the car. They're looking across the street at an alley. I follow Gray's gaze, and there he is. Dimitri is standing in the alley in the shadows with someone behind him. Watching and smiling. He's looking right at Gray. As I watch, too stunned to move, he reaches behind him and holds up a phone.

I see Gray reach into their pocket, and I stumble to stand beside them. My balance is off from the explosion's impact on my inner ear, and it takes me a moment to gain my feet and get over to Gray.

As I approach Gray, I hear, "Fuck you, Dimitri." Every

word ground out through their clenched teeth. The hand holding the phone is white, and Gray grips it tightly.

"If you fucking touch them …"

I can't hear what Dimitri is saying, but I can see from where I'm standing that he has a huge smile as he hangs up and tosses the phone. He turns to leave, and I start to move toward him.

"Kee, no! We have to get to the house." Gray's words cut through the weird fog that's filled my mind.

The house?

I turn, and my feet start moving toward Gray before my brain fully catches up. I'm soon racing behind them as we go for our vehicle.

"I need everyone to get back to the house! They're going after Hannah and Marcus! Anyone available needs to get there now!" Gray shouts as we both sprint toward our SUV. I hear responses over the earpiece, but the voices I don't hear concern me more.

"I need someone to get eyes on Luke and James! They were near the explosions."

"I'm here with them!" Neko's voice relieves me, knowing they're safe and in good hands. "They were both caught in the explosion, but I think they should be fine. I'm transporting them to the hospital now."

"Keep me updated, Neko," I say, slamming into the side of the SUV and yanking the door open.

"Everyone on me when we get to the house. Nobody moves until we're all there and get a read on the situation. Understand?" Gray says, flinging the driver-side door open.

"Copies" ring through my earpiece, and Gray slams on the gas, deftly navigating through the chaos toward Hannah's house. My heart is in my throat.

I can't lose either of them.

# CHAPTER 32

## Marcus

Everything goes wrong at once.

The screens around Hannah and I go dark as there's a knock at the front door, and my phone goes off in my pocket. What the fuck is going on?

Hannah gets up to go to the front door before I can stop her, and I reach for my phone, desperate to stop the annoying vibration.

The screen says "Kee", which I find weird, considering they should all be busy with the caravan about now.

I'm slow to put things together, but as I pick up the call, hear Kee's rushed voice, and look at the dark screens, it comes together. I'm too late, though, and just as I turn to warn Hannah, the house's front door is violently pushed open, knocking Hannah onto her back in the hallway.

"Hannah!" I roar and run to the front of the house as fast as my weakened body will allow me.

"Don't fucking move, Marcus!" Kiera is there with her unfortunate sidekick, Vlad. They're both looking snide and happy with themselves as they stride into the townhouse, shutting and locking the doors behind them.

Fuck. This is not good.

I stutter to a stop halfway down the hall. Hannah lies sprawled between us. Kiera and Vlad have guns; I cannot move without endangering her.

My lips instinctively peel back in a snarl as I look at them. Hannah is scuttling backward toward me as Kiera strides into the hall.

"Have you both missed me?"

"Go fuck yourself, Kiera." I reach down, helping Hannah to her feet as she reaches my side.

"How rude. I've missed you both terribly and can't wait to have fun with you!" Kiera stalks forward with Vlad at her side.

I place myself before Hannah, whispering as I pass her, "Get ready to run."

With every step that Kiera and Vlad take forward, I take two back, pushing Hannah back as I go. If we can get close to the sunroom, she'll have a chance to run for it while I distract Kiera and Vlad.

If she can get out, there's a chance that Hannah will be able to get help, and Kiera won't have as much time as she thinks she has.

We continue backing down the hallway, only a few steps from the sunroom.

I give Hannah a slight push and block her from view so she can continue to move back without being seen.

Now, I need to keep their focus.

"I heard they caught your dad before he could escape. That sounds about right. You and your dad can't seem to do anything right."

There's a slight flare behind Kiera's eyes, but it's soon tampered as she smiles, baring her teeth.

"Don't try to fool me, Marcus. I've already heard from my father, and he's long gone by now. I believe he took out a few of your friends in the process. Sadly, your lovely Kee may not have made it."

Now it's my turn to snarl. Just hearing Kee's name from her mouth pisses me off.

"Don't even mention Kee," I growl, instinctively moving toward Kiera. Vlad steps closer to her side, and we all notice Hannah is no longer in the hallway.

"Where is she?!" Kiera yells, storming forward, Vlad trailing beside her like the lost dog he is.

My lips peel back in a feral grin.

"Looks like your dad isn't the only one that got away."

I launch myself at Kiera, hoping to catch both off guard.

Vlad is faster than he looks, stepping in front of Kiera and catching my swing. He pushes me back, and I stumble, my ribs and broken bones screaming in protest.

Kiera levels the gun at me. "Don't try that again, Marcus. Get on your knees, now!"

Staring down the barrel of her gun, I slowly drop to my knees, and Vlad walks around behind me, zip-tying my hands before moving to the sunroom to look for Hannah. I can only hope that she's had enough time to get out.

Kiera asks me, "Shall we have some fun, Marcus? Like old times?" She smiles, and chills run down my spine.

# CHAPTER 33

## Kee

Gray and I screech to a halt down the block from Hannah's house. God, it was stupid of us to think that they would be safe here.

We both get out of the car and bolt down the street. The rest of our security team is nowhere to be seen, and I fear the worst has happened to them. Gray slows in front of me and pulls out their gun. I follow suit, drawing my Glock from its holster and making sure the safety is off.

We take cover behind a car parked just in front of the house.

"What's the plan?" I ask breathlessly.

"I'm not sure. The front door looks intact, but I can hear voices occasionally, so I know they're in there."

"We need to move." I get up, but Gray pulls me back behind the car.

"What are you doing? We can't wait for Marcus and Hannah to be there with Kiera! Who knows what she's doing to them." I pull away from Gray and start toward the building again before being pulled back by Gray.

"Kee, Kee! Listen to me! I know you want to rush in

there. Trust me, I do too. Every fiber wants to run into that house and ensure that Hannah and Marcus are okay, but we must be smart about this. We know that Kiera has Vlad and access to the explosives she brought back with her from Russia. She could have rigged the front door. There's no telling what they've had time to do, so we need to be smart about this."

Gray lets go of my arm and looks at me, pleading for me to understand.

Taking a deep breath, I nod and settle beside them behind the car, and that's when I see Hannah.

"What the fuck?!" I point, and Gray runs to her before I can stop them.

"Hannah. Hannah," Gray whispers loudly for her and moves to meet her as she runs from the house toward the car. Gray grabs Hannah's hand, pulling her close.

The three of us embrace each other. Gray holds Hannah's face in their hands and checks her for injuries as I watch the front of the house.

"I'm okay, I'm okay," Hannah whispers, holding onto Gray, grounding herself and Gray.

"How did you get out?" Gray asks, looking from Hannah to the front of the house.

"Marcus. He put himself between us and helped me get out of the sunroom. He bought me time by distracting Kiera and Vlad so I could sneak out before they even noticed anything was happening." Hannah starts to shake as she shares how she escaped, and it's clear that the event has her stunned.

"Can you tell us anything about Kiera and Vlad that we need to know before we go in? How were they armed? Did they have any explosives?" Gray's trying to be gentle, but we also need the information to help Marcus.

"No ... no explosives. They both had guns, though.

Gray, Kiera is … insane. I'm really worried for Marcus. There's no telling what she'll do."

"It's okay. Kee and I will get him out of there."

I nod as Gray says this and look back at the front of the house, "Gray, we should make our move quickly before they have time to do anything else." Gray nods and turns back to Hannah.

"Hannah, you stay here. If any team members show up, tell them what you told us and let them know that we've gone in through the sunroom in the back of the house. Do you understand?"

Hannah nods, and Gray and I pick our way to the small alley between the townhomes, using cars for cover.

It's dangerous for us to go in without backup, but the longer we wait, the longer Kiera and Vlad have to rig the house and hurt Marcus.

We have to make our move now before it's too late.

# CHAPTER 34

## Marcus

Vlad roughly lifts me to my feet. It hurts like a bitch as my injuries flare, and it's hard not to flinch in pain. I don't want to show weakness, but my already battered body won't sustain much this time.

Vlad pushes me away from the sunroom and toward the living room where Kiera has set up shop. They've closed all the blinds, and Kiera is lounging casually on the sofa as if she's over for Sunday tea.

"Sit, Marcus." She motions to the floor in front of her, and Vlad obliges her by kicking the back of my knee, causing me to go down to both knees with a thump.

I close my eyes as pain screams through my body.

I breathe, trying to steady myself as I'm reminded of the last time I found myself in Kiera's hands. I can't go through that again. There's no way I'll be able to withstand the same type of torture that I've already been through.

I can't do this again.

The panic sets in as I look up at Kiera and see her smiling back at me.

"Thinking about the old times, Marcus? You'll be happy

to know I've learned new tricks since we last saw each other. I think you'll enjoy them. Vlad, check the sunroom and ensure it's secure before we start with Marcus here."

Vlad nods and lumbers away toward the back of the house. At least Hannah got out. That's good. I'm glad Gray will have Hannah there for them if I can't be around. Gray and Hannah deserve to be happy, and Gray needs someone they can lean on and trust.

My mind wanders to Kee as Kiera stands up and moves toward me. I feel a lot of regrets when it comes to Kee. I regret not sticking around and being with her for longer, not letting her fully get to know me, and leaving her like this. I hate that this is how she'll remember me, broken and alone. She only saw me at my best for a brief moment before everything with Dimitri and Kiera started. We could have been something great if only this hadn't happened.

I look up at Kiera as she stands over me. I feel the prickling of tears in the corners of my eyes as I realize everything, I will be missing with Kee.

"Poor Marcus, you can't seem to stay away from me." Kiera holds up a small knife and crouches before me so our faces are on the same level. "I'd hate to mess up such a handsome face, but you need a reminder that I'm always with you. Just like the one that Father and I gave Gray."

Kiera places the small blade on my face, under my eye, and runs the impeccably sharp edge across my cheek parallel to my eye. I hiss in pain but manage to hold the scream in. As Kiera laughs in glee, I can feel the warm blood sliding down my face and hear it splattering on the cold wood floor.

Kiera doesn't hear the thud that comes from down the hall. It's barely audible, and I almost missed it myself. But it was there. Someone else must be in the house. I hope it's Gray and the rest of the team.

I let myself hope that there's a way out of this.

# CHAPTER 35

## Kee

Gray and I move to the back of the house, sticking to the shadows. My heart is beating so loudly that I'm afraid Keira and Vlad will be able to hear it. I take a steadying breath and follow close on Gray's heels as they move forward.

I trust Gray to take the lead because I know Marcus means as much to them as he does to me. I also know that Gray and Marcus have been partners for years and can read each other's moves better than I can. They know what each other is thinking, and that's invaluable.

We move to the back door of the sunroom, and Gray opens it slowly. The brightly lit room is empty, and while still bright, the air and space are tense. We move into the room.

I grab Gray's arm and motion for them to listen.

There it is, the creak of the floor in the hall. Someone is coming our way.

Gray may know Marcus better than I, but I know this house. I've spent the last year in this house going over every inch, knowing every floor creak and where all the shadows are. I know that sound, and it means someone is headed our direction.

We move simultaneously to the wall to have a clear line on whoever enters the room. Gray holsters their weapon and readies for what's coming next.

Vlad walks in.

He's monstrous and towers over us, coming in at least six-foot-six or taller. He's all muscle, and Gray gulps as they launch at him. Trying to get him in a chokehold before he can react.

It doesn't go as planned, and before I know it, Gray is sprawled across the sunroom floor, having been tossed aside by Vlad.

Hopefully, Kiera doesn't hear any of this.

I pick up the closest chair and swing at Vlad as he closes the distance between us. The chair catches him across the side of his face, and he stumbles but doesn't go down. I go to hit him again, and he grabs the chair. Gray goes in for the chokehold again as we fight for control over my makeshift weapon. This time, Gray locks it in and uses their legs, locking them around his waist and arching backward for extra leverage.

Vlad ditches his efforts of holding onto the chair and grapples with Gray's hold. I lock eyes with Gray, whose face is bright red from the effort, and give them a nod, indicating that I'm about to bash Vlad's head in with this chair.

Gray pulls their face away but doesn't let go. We can't risk it. I raise the chair above my head and bring it down on Vlad's head again. A piece of the wooden frame splinters, cutting Gray's arm and face.

Vlad slumps backward, landing on Gray, crushing them with his unconscious weight.

"Hurry and tie his hands," they mumble from under him.

I pull out the zip ties we carry in our gear, and together, we roll him over, tying his hands behind his back.

"We also need to gag him," Gray whispers breathlessly.

"Sorry, Hannah," I whisper under my breath. I nod, grab one of the blankets from the couch, and tear off a piece of the corner to use as a gag.

Vlad, now bound and gagged, is out of the way. Kiera is the only thing left between getting to Marcus.

Gray and I make our move. I'm leading now and slink silently down the hall, avoiding all the places that will give us away to prying ears.

I hear Kiera mocking Marcus from the living room and stick to the closest wall as Gray moves to the wall across from me. We look at each other, counting down silently before bursting into the living room, guns drawn and targeting Kiera.

"Don't fucking move, Kiera!" Gray shouts as they move forward, coming up along my side.

My breath catches as I see Marcus. A deep cut runs horizontally across his face, and a small pool of blood forms on the floor before him. I don't see any other wounds, but the haunted look in his eyes is enough to make me take a step forward.

Gray moves with me, and we both stand across from Kiera, who stands, pointing her gun directly at Marcus.

"Don't do anything stupid, Kiera. This is over. You have no escape this time."

"If either of you moves, I will put a bullet in him." Kiera snarls and presses the gun harder into Marcus' temple.

I can't stop the growl that comes from me as she does. Everything in me is screaming to get to Marcus, to help him. If that means taking Kiera out, it's something I'm willing to do.

"Kiera, think about it. You get nothing from killing

him. You can't escape this situation. There's no way out for you. Just put the gun down and come with us."

"Oh, I get plenty from this! I get to take away a person who means so much to both of you in one go. I'll die knowing that I took that person from you and that you'll have to live the rest of your lives knowing that you couldn't do anything to stop it."

Kiera is spiraling, and we can both see it. Her finger presses on the trigger, and Gray and I both pull the trigger in that split second.

Our bullets slam into Kiera's body simultaneously, ripping the gun from her hands and flinging her backward onto the couch. Marcus instinctively drops to the ground in case Kiera's gun goes off.

I rush to his side as Gray checks Kiera.

"She's gone," Gray says softly. Even though it was Kiera or Marcus, killing someone is not ideal. I glance at Kiera's lifeless body with a wave of regret and sadness.

I kneel in front of Marcus, pulling him up and holding his face. Gray moves away, then to the front door.

I know things are happening around us, but my only focus is on Marcus, and everything else fades away.

"Are you okay?" I ask him, holding a dish towel to the cut on his face. He'll need stitches and likely have a scar, but considering what the outcome could have been, he got off lightly.

"Yeah, yeah, I'm alright," he whispers, moving his hands to brace my shoulders before pulling me into a crushing hug.

"I'm sorry I've been so distant, and I'm sorry that I left without saying anything. I'm so sorry." The words come pouring out of Marcus on a breath of rushed air as he clings to me.

I'm still pressing the towel to his face as he captures me, and I squeeze him back the best I can, resting my head on his shoulder and enjoying the feel of his body against mine.

"I've missed you so much, Marcus. I'm glad you've come back to me again." I pull away just enough to brush my lips over his.

He smiles back at me, wincing as I help him onto his feet. Gray is already outside with the rest of the team and the authorities. Hannah is right there by their side, checking on Gray's wounds. When she sees Marcus, she rushes forward.

"Oh, Marcus, are you okay? Let me see!" Hannah reaches for the towel, but I stop her. "It's okay, Hannah. We'll head directly to the hospital to get him patched up. I'll let you know what the verdict is."

"Okay, let me know if you need anything. I'm sure we won't be far behind you."

Nodding, I take Marcus' hand and lead him to one of the SUVs. I help him in and then walk around to the driver's side door. Only then do I look around again and notice that James and Luke are missing.

I catch Neko's eye. "Where are James and Luke? Are they okay?"

"They both caught shrapnel from the explosion and are at the hospital. You'll find Mika there with them. I think they're both going to be okay. James might have a longer recovery, but they'll be okay."

"Shit, okay. Thanks, Neko."

I grab the door handle and get into the SUV, instinctively reaching for Marcus' hand after I shift into drive.

"What was that about?"

"Luke and James were caught in the blast and are at the hospital. I'll check on them and Finn while we're there." I look at Marcus, and an overwhelming sense of relief surrounds me. It's so intense that I almost have to pull the vehicle over as my eyes get blurry.

"It's alright, I'm alright," Marcus whispers.

Nodding, I keep driving. Arriving at the hospital, we

head into the ER. Cassie, Hannah's friend, is waiting for us at the door.

"Hannah called ahead and said you need some patching up. I'm beginning to think Hannah is hanging out with the wrong crowd. Y'all are in here *way* too much!" Cassie gives us a joking smile and walks us into the ER.

They already have a plastic surgeon on call in case they're needed. As Marcus settles onto the table and they start examining him, I wander off, searching for James.

"Excuse me, can you tell me what room James Adamo is in?" The nurse points me in the right direction, and we now have our little corner in the hospital's recovery area. They've put James, Luke, and Finn all in the same corner, making it easy for me to check in on them.

I pop into James's room first. He's out cold and looks like hell. He's definitely seen better days.

He's got a bandage around his head, several bandages on his face covering cuts, and it looks like one of his arms is in a sling.

I don't want to wake him, so I slowly leave the room, poking my head in on Luke next. He's in a similar state with fewer bumps and bruises. One of his legs is in a boot. They must have been closer than I thought when the explosion happened.

Backing out of his room, I head to Finn's. He's sitting up in bed and looking more aware than he has since he was shot, helping us rescue Marcus.

"Hi Finn, we've never met, but thank you for helping us get Marcus back." I walk into the room and hold my hand out for the younger man to shake.

He's pale still, making his brownish-red hair stand out starkly against his skin.

"You're Kee. You must be. Luke told us about you and Marcus. I'm glad we were able to recover him. I'm sorry all of this happened to the both of you." He has a slight southern drawl and tremendous kindness behind his light blue eyes.

"Thank you, Finn, really. For everything that you've given to us."

He smiles, looking down, and a faint dusting of red colors on his pale cheeks. "It's no problem at all."

Smiling back at him, I clasp his hand, thank him again, and head back to where Marcus is.

Standing back and watching Marcus, I'm suddenly hit with how much I love this man. It's overwhelming how much I want and need him.

Marcus catches my eyes and smiles, sending butterflies through my entire body.

This time, we're heading back to my place.

# CHAPTER 36

## Marcus

It's been a few days since Kiera and Vlad broke into Hannah's home.

I finally feel like I'm getting back to myself, and the rest of the team is also slowly recovering. Finn is leaving the hospital this week and will be heading back to the team along with Luke and James. I'm glad that everyone is recovering well.

Kee is back to watching Hannah's place since Dimitri escaped again. They have a few leads, but the DEA can't seem to get a handle on him, which makes me worried. We killed his daughter, after all; if someone is out to get revenge, it will be Dimitri. Gray's trying to convince Hannah that she may have to move again or stay in a safe house until they catch him.

I'm sitting on the end of the bed in Kee's house, thinking about the last several weeks when she walks in. I've been staying with her while recovering, and we've got a nice routine, but I will be moving to stay at Hannah's place soon.

"You ready for bed already, old man?" Kee asks playfully.

"I'm ready for you in this bed." I hold out my hand for her. Kee's playfulness changes to that of a different kind.

Her breathing quickens, and I can see the pulse in her neck jump as I pull her to me.

I pull her legs onto the bed so she's straddling my lap, and I grip her thighs lightly to hold her in place.

"Can I?" I ask breathlessly, staring longingly at her lips.

"Please," she whispers back.

I pull her forward and take her mouth with mine. First, I gently brush my lips over hers before deepening the kiss, sliding my tongue across her lips and asking permission to enter. She opens her mouth more, giving me access, and I lose myself in the feeling of her.

I pull her sweater off over her head and am rewarded with the beauty of her strong, beautiful body. Every piece of me wants to be with her at this moment and all moments moving forward.

As my hands roam down her stunning body, I pepper kisses down her neck, nuzzling where her collarbone connects with her sternum at the base. I cup her ass with one hand while the other slips the cup of her bra down over one of her breasts. I kiss my way to her nipple and run my tongue over it as it pebbles under my touch.

"Marcus …" Her torn whisper makes me harder as I press into her.

Kee pulls my shirt off over my head and reaches down to unbutton my pants. I pull her bra the rest of the way down, exposing her breasts as she writhes against me. Our panting mingles as we undress one another.

We stand so we can disrobe the rest of the way, parting only long enough to come back together fully naked.

Our bodies mold together as one as we tumble back onto the bed.

I sink into her and feel her wrap around me as she rides me. I'm close as she leans down to kiss me, increasing the rhythm. I feel my way down her body as she leans back, losing herself in the sensation. My hands find the places she needs to find her release.

"Kee … I'm going to come soon." The broken words whisper as she clenches around me, urging me to come.

"Marcus …" she whispers again as she feels my release and grips harder still.

Tumbling to the bed, we lay in the tangled sheets, entirely spent.

"Can we stay like this forever?" Kee asks, rolling into me and laying her head and hand on my chest.

"I definitely think that's doable," I whisper, kissing her.

Preview of We All Fall

# CHAPTER 1

## James

My world slowly comes into focus as the ringing in my ears grows louder. I can't seem to draw a breath, and something is wrong with my arm. It doesn't want to move even though I'm telling it to. I try to roll to my side and can't even manage. I gasp for air and stare up at the cloudy sky. No, it's not cloudy. It's smoky. Smoke, that's right, something exploded. I must have been close to whatever it was.

I try to lift my head, which seems to weigh more than it should. I look down at my body, taking account of my injuries as my head begins to clear a bit. My arm is completely fucked. I can see the bone sticking out of the flesh of my forearm, but I can't seem to feel anything.

I try to roll to my side again and manage to get my good arm under me so that I can prop myself up. A dull noise comes from in front of me, but I can't register what it is. All I can do is focus on pulling rapid, sooty breaths into my heaving lungs.

The sound sharpens, and I look up as Neko grabs my shoulders, "James, hey, James! You're alright, I've got you.

Where's Luke?" Neko is looking around and has ash in his hair.

It looks like snow.

My brain must really be scrambled. I can't seem to focus on anything he's saying. His mouth is moving, and I know he's talking to me, but nothing makes sense.

"James! Let's get you up and see if we can find Luke."

Luke?

Where was Luke? Was he nearby when the explosion happened?

"What…what exploded?" I manage to get the words out of my oddly dry mouth. I cough as I choke on my words.

"Two cars in the caravan, Dimitri, got away, and Kiera has Hannah and Marcus."

"What?" I mumble as Neko helps me to my feet. I feel like I'm on a boat in rocky waters. The world swims in and out of focus as I rock unsteadily on my feet.

"Take it slow, man." Neko has a tight grip on my upper arm and has somehow secured my injured arm in a make-shift sling.

When did he do that?

"Where's Luke?" I ask, suddenly overcome with a large amount of concern for the younger man.

"I don't know. I haven't seen him since the explosion."

Looking around, I see the corner where he was standing before the car exploded. Pointing in that direction, Neko helps me walk toward where Luke once was.

"Do you see him anywhere?" I choke out, still coughing around my seemingly swollen tongue.

Maybe I bit it when I was blown backward by the explosion.

Neko turns to answer me when I glimpse a booted foot just barely visible from underneath a pile of debris.

"Neko, there." My voice sounds oddly hollow and dead in my ears as I look at the dusty and scuffed boot.

The laces are undone.

"Stay right here," Neko says and jogs over to where the body is.

I can't stay here.

I stumble forward, and with what little strength I have left, I help Neko remove the debris from off of the person beneath it. As the last bit of what looks like part of the car's hood comes off, I see Luke's blonde hair, and everything seems to freeze.

He looks like he's asleep.

Neko kneels over Luke, checking for a pulse, before taking his belt off to make a tourniquet above a wound on his lower leg. As he tightens the belt, a gasp from Luke draws my eyes to his face, and his bright blue eyes find mine.

"James?"

"I'm here, Luke, I'm right here."

"What's going on?" Luke's voice is raspy and barely audible.

"The caravan exploded," Neko repeats what he's already told me to Luke as he looks him over.

My strength gives out, and I plop down next to Luke, still heaving in breaths of ash-laden air as it settles around us.

"Are you okay?" Luke asks as Neko continues to look him over and triage his wounds.

I can't bring myself to talk, so I simply nod. I zone out, disconnecting, trying to stop the memories from returning. A touch on my hand brings me back to reality. Luke is still lying on his back but has reached over and is tentatively holding onto my hand. I look from his blood and dust-covered face to our hands and try to process what's happening, but my brain is lagging, and I can't. Everything is still swimming, and I think I've blown an eardrum as I can't hear very well.

It reminds me of before, of the last explosion I was in, and I feel the panic creeping up in my gut, taking hold of my already struggling lungs and turning my muscles into tightened ropes.

"James? James!" Luke tightens his hold on my hand, and I glance at him. His eyes are brighter than usual, with the dark red of the blood and gray of the dust making them pop against his paler skin.

"I asked if you were okay," Luke says again. I focus on his lips as I try to understand and comprehend what he's saying.

The ringing in my ears has started to lessen, but my head feels cloudy and heavy. I must have hit it pretty hard.

I nod, looking Luke in the eyes, then glancing down at his prone body to where Neko is still working on his wounded lower leg. I can't bring myself to ask if Luke is okay.

"I'm fine." He says as if he can read my mind, "I'm fine, James. Take a deep breath, just breathe." He squeezes my hand again, and I draw a full breath, forcing it into my tight lungs. In through my nose, out through my mouth, just like they teach us.

I nod again and look away to take in the wreckage around us. The street has been cleared, and all that remains are the remnants of the burnt-out cars and the bodies of those impacted by the explosion. Myself and Luke included.

Neko stands suddenly, drawing my attention away from the destruction around us. He's waving his arms over his head and yelling. I can barely hear his yelling, so I look at Luke.

"The team is going to transport us to the hospital. Some of them went with Gray and Kee to deal with Kiera." I nod again, feeling the weight of my head as I move it. Maybe I shouldn't be moving it so much. I take my hand away from Luke, sliding it along the rubble-covered road, and bring it to my head. I feel along my scalp and find a large gash on the back of my head that is leaking blood.

That'll do it.

I pull my hand away and look at it. The flashback happens out of nowhere. Suddenly, I'm sitting in the sand, surrounded by the remains of a building that exploded. My hands are covered in the violent red of his blood as it spills from his body. Shawn lays motionless in my arms as I try to stem the bleeding, but there's too much damage, too much blood. How can the human body have that much blood in it?

My ears are full of the sounds of gunfire around me, the popping and whizzing of the bullets hitting the ground and building rubble behind me as I sit there, unable to leave him as he gasps his last breath. His blue eyes look into mine as the light dims from them, leaving behind light bluish-gray sightless orbs.

Shawn.

A hand on my shoulder pulls me out of the flashback, and Neko's face fills my vision, "James? Dude, you must be more fucked up than I thought. I need you to get up and walk for me. Can you do that?"

I glance to where Luke was only to find that he's no longer there. I follow the trail of blood to one of the SUVs that's parked a few feet away.

"Come on, let's get you to the hospital and get you checked out."

I let Neko help me up and lean on him to keep my balance as I stumble over charred car bits. He guides me to the back of the SUV, where they've laid down the second row of seats to make enough room for Luke and me to lie down.

Neko helps me crawl into the back next to where Luke

is already lying. I let out a sigh as soon as I settle in and start to close my eyes.

"You need to stay awake." Luke says Neko agrees as he shuts the door, "That's right, James, no sleeping. Stay awake. Luke, talk to him."

The door shuts, and a few seconds later, we're bumping along the road to the hospital where Hannah works. We're there too often.

As if reading my thoughts, Luke says, "Do you think they get tired of seeing us at the hospital?"

I'm not sure if I can trust my voice, but I manage to croak a weak "Yes." And fight the urge to sleep. It's getting more challenging with the vehicle rocking and the white noise still filling my ears.

"Hey, James, you have to stay awake. You've probably got a nasty concussion." Luke reaches over and holds my hand again. I fight the urge to pull my hand away. Maybe Luke is feeling scared and needs some reassurance. I can do that for him. I can let him hold my hand. It doesn't mean anything else.

I breathe in through my nose and out through my mouth several times, dragging cold air into my parched lungs.

"You going to be alright?" Luke's voice has softened, and he tightens his grip on my hand.

"Yeah, I'll be okay. I'm just dizzy." I can't open my eyes without the world swimming and swirling around me. I definitely have a concussion, maybe the worst one I've ever experienced.

"Just as long as you're not sleeping, you can keep your eyes shut. But I need you to talk to me." A small groan escapes from Luke's tightly clenched lips, reminding me that he's also been hurt.

I turn my head tentatively and look at the man lying next to me in the back of the SUV, "Are you going to be okay?" I'm scared to ask, what if he's not but thinks he is. What if Luke's injuries are worse than they seem?

His face is still covered in blood and soot and pale, but the light is back in his blue eyes. His long blonde hair is matted to his head in spots where he was hit with shrapnel and is no longer in the man bun that it started off in.

I try to raise my head to look at his leg but can't. It's just so damn heavy.

"Your leg?" I manage.

"It'll be fine. I mean, I think it will be. It's pretty fucked up, kinda like your arm, but I think it'll be fine." There's trepidation in his voice, and when I open my eyes again, he's looking down at his leg, uncertainty written across his face.

I squeeze his hand, and he looks over, meeting my eyes.

"We'll get through this," Luke says, giving me one of his smirks.

How can he always be so positive?

Shawn was like that, too. So cheerful and…light.

Fuck, I can't think about Shawn, I haven't thought about him in so long, but today is dredging up all of the memories and feelings that I've had safely buried for years.

The air in my lungs catches, and I feel like I'm choking for a second before I force the air out again in a little hiccup. I'm panicking again. I know the feeling all too well and try to control it with my breathing before it takes over.

"James?" Luke props himself up while looking at my face.

I close my eyes and concentrate on my breathing.

"I'm fine." I force it out between my teeth.

"What's happening right now?" He asks, his hand leaving mine to settle on my shoulder.

"Nothing, nothing is happening, I'm all good." I would roll away from him if I could, but the very thought of moving makes my body ache in protest.

"You're not *all good*," Luke says, concern obvious in his tone.

"I'll be fine. I need a minute to catch my breath."

"Did you break a rib or something?" He goes to feel my ribs as if that will make it better.

"No, my ribs are fine. I just need a fucking minute, okay." I can hear the frustration and anger in my voice, making me even more frustrated that I've snapped at Luke.

"Sorry, I'm just…I'm sorry. I didn't mean to snap." I try to open my eyes, but Luke's swimming face and the look of hurt on it makes me close them immediately before it makes me ill.

"No worries, man. You do you. I was trying to help." Luke settles back, removes his hand from my shoulder, and lays it across his stomach, far from my hand.

I stretch my fingers out as if I could catch his hand from where I'm lying, but I know I've pushed him away with my outburst. I know that he's just worried for me and that I should appreciate his care. I know all this, but I can do nothing when the panic hits. It consumes me. Takes over everything, and I can barely manage myself, and he was asking so many questions.

I feel like I could sob, feel like I could let myself fall apart right here. But I don't. I can't. That's not who I'm supposed to be.

I swallow my pain, panic, and feelings and let the moments pass, trying not to feel bad but knowing that I've really fucked up this time.

POINT YOUR PHONE AND SCAN
THE QR CODE AND GET 10% OFF
ON THE NEXT BOOK IN THE FALL
SERIES!

www.ardencoutts.com

www.ardencoutts.com